The Hundred Best
English Poems

Various
Edited by Adam L. Gowans

The Hundred Best English Poems

Copyright © 2023 Bibliotech Press
All rights reserved

The present edition is a reproduction of previous publication of this classic work. Minor typographical errors may have been corrected without note; however, for an authentic reading experience the spelling, punctuation, and capitalization have been retained from the original text.

ISBN: 979-8-88830-682-6

PREFATORY NOTE

Let me frankly admit, to begin with, that the attractiveness and probable selling qualities of the title of this little book, "The Hundred Best English Poems," proved, when it had been once thought of, too powerful arguments for it to be abandoned. I am fully conscious of the presumption such a title implies in an unknown selector, but at the same time I submit that only a plebiscite of duly qualified lovers of poetry could make a selection that could claim to deserve this title beyond all question, and such a plebiscite is of course impossible. I can claim no more than that my attempt to realize this title is an honest one, and I can assert, without fear of contradiction, that every one of the poems I have included is a "gem of purest ray serene"; that none can be too often read or too often repeated to one's self; that every one of them should be known by heart by every lover of good literature, so that each may become, as it were, a part of his inner being.

I have not inserted any poems by living authors.

I have taken the greatest care with the texts of the poems. The editions followed have been mentioned in every case. I have scrupulously retained the punctuation of these original editions, and only modernized the spelling of the old copies; while I have not ventured to omit any part of any poem. I have not supplied titles of my own, but have adopted those I found already employed in the editions used as models, or, in some of the cases in which I found none, have merely added a descriptive one, such as "Song from 'Don Juan.'"

In conclusion, my very warmest thanks are due to Messrs. Macmillan & Co., Ltd., for permission to include Tennyson's "Crossing the Bar"; to Mr. D. Nutt for permission to insert W. E. Henley's "To R. T. H. B." and "Margaritae Sorori"; to Messrs. Smith,

Elder & Co. for a like privilege in regard to Browning's "Epilogue," and to Mr. Lloyd Osbourne and Messrs. Chatto & Windus for permission to reproduce Stevenson's "Requiem." Without these poems the volume would have had a much smaller claim to its title than it does possess, slight as that may be. My thanks are also due to the following gentlemen who have kindly allowed me to reproduce copyright texts of non-copyright poems from editions published by them: Messrs. Bickers & Son (Ben Jonson), Messrs. Chapman & Hall, Ltd. (Landor), Messrs. Chatto & Windus (Herrick), Mr. Buxton Forman (Keats and Shelley), Mr. Henry Frowde (Wordsworth), Mr. Alex. Gardner and the Rev. George Henderson, B.D. (Lady Nairne), Messrs. T. C. & E. C. Jack (Burns), Messrs. Macmillan & Co., Ltd. (Clough and Tennyson), Mr. John Murray (Byron), Messrs. Smith, Elder & Co. (Browning), Messrs. Ward, Lock & Co., Ltd. (Coleridge and Hood).

A. L. G.

CONTENTS

Anonymous
1. Madriga 1
Arnold (1822-1888)
2. The Forsaken Merman 1
Barbauld (1743-1825)
3. Life 7
Browning (1812-1889)
4. Song from "Pippa Passes" 8
5. Song from "Pippa Passes" 8
6. The Lost Mistress 9
7. Home-Thoughts, from the Sea 10
8. Epilogue 10
Burns (1759-1796)
9. The Silver Tassie 11
10. Of a' the Airts 11
11. John Anderson my Jo 12
12. Ae Fond Kiss 13
13. Ye Flowery Banks 14
14. A Red, Red Rose 15
15. Mary Morison 16
Byron (1788-1824)
16. She Walks in Beauty 17
17. Oh! Snatched Away in Beauty's Bloom 18
18. Song from "The Corsair" 19
19. Song from "Don Juan" 20
Campbell (1777-1844)
20. Hohenlinden 24
Clough (1819-1861)
21. Say not the Struggle Nought Availeth 25
Coleridge (1772-1834)
22. Youth and Age 26

v

Collins (1721-1759)
23. Written in the Year 1746 28
Cowper (1731-1800)
24. To a Young Lady 28
Cunningham (1784-1842)
25. A Wet Sheet and a Flowing Sea 29
Davenant (1606-1668)
26. Song 30
Dryden (1631-1700)
27. A Song for St. Cecilia's Day, 1687 30
Goldsmith (1728-1774)
28. Song 33
Gray (1716-1771)
29. Elegy written in a Country Church-yard 33
Henley (1849-1903)
30. To R. T. H. B. 38
31. I. M. Margaritae Sorori 39
Herbert (1593-1632)
32. Virtue 40
Herrick (1591-1674)
33. To the Virgins, to make much of Time 41
34. To Anthea, who may command him anything 42
Hood (1798-1845)
35. The Death Bed 43
36. The Bridge of Sighs 43
37. I Remember, I Remember 47
Jonson (1573-1637)
38. To Celia 48
Keats (1795-1821)
39. On first looking into Chapman's Homer 49
40. Ode to a Nightingale 49
41. Ode on a Grecian Urn 52
42. To Autumn 54
43. Ode on Melancholy 55
44. La Belle Dame sans Merci 56
45. Sonnet 58
Lamb (1775-1834)
46. The Old Familiar Faces 58
Landor (1775-1864)
47. The Maid's Lament 60
Lovelace (1618-1658)
48. To Lucasta. Going to the Wars 61

Milton (1608-1674)

49. On the Morning of Christ's Nativity 61
50. L'Allegro 70
51. Il Penseroso 74
52. Lycidas 79
53. On his Blindness 84

Nairine (1766-1845)

54. The Land o' the Leal 85

Pope (1688-1744)

55. Ode on Solitude 86

Raleigh (1552-1618)

56. The Night before his Death 87

Rogers (1763-1855)

57. A Wish 87

Shakespeare (1564-1616)

58. Sonnets. XVII. Who will believe my verse? 88
59. XVIII. Shall I compare thee to a summer's day? 89
60. XXX. When to the sessions 89
61. XXXIII. Full many a glorious morning 90
62. LX. Like as the waves 90
63. LXVI. Tired with all these 91
64. LXXI. No longer mourn 91
65. LXXIII. That time of year 92
66. LXXIV. But be contented 92
67. CVI. When in the chronicle 93
68. CXVI. Let me not to the marriage 93
69. Song from "The Tempest" 94
70. Song from "Measure for Measure" 94
71. Song from "Much Ado about Nothing" 94
72. Song from "Cymbeline" 95

Shelley (1792-1822)

73. Song from "Prometheus Unbound" 96
74. Ode to the West Wind 96
75. The Cloud 99
76. To a Skylark 102
77. Chorus from "Hellas" 105
78. Stanzas. Written in Dejection, near Naples 107
79. The Indian Serenade 108
80. To —— 109
81. To Night 110

Shirley (1596-1666)

82. Song from "Ajax and Ulysses" 111

vii

Southey (1774-1843)
83. Stanzas 112

Stevenson (1850-1894)
84. Requiem 113

Tennyson (1809-1892)
85. Song from "The Miller's Daughter" 113
86. St. Agnes' Eve 114
87. Break, break, break 115
88. Song from "The Princess" 116
89. Song from "The Princess" 117
90. Crossing the Bar 117

Waller (1606-1687)
91. On a Girdle 118
92. Song 118

Wordsworth (1770-1850)
93. She dwelt among the untrodden ways 119
94. She was a Phantom of delight 120
95. Sonnets. Part I.—XXXIII. The world is too much
with us 121
96. Part II.—XXXVI. Earth has not anything 121
97. To a Highland Girl, at Inversneyde, upon Loch
Lomond 122
98. The Solitary Reaper 124
99. Intimations of Immortality from Recollections of
Early Childhood 125

Wotton (1568-1639)
100. On his Mistress, the Queen of Bohemia 132

THE HUNDRED BEST
ENGLISH POEMS

ANONYMOUS

1. Madrigal

Love not me for comely grace,
For my pleasing eye or face;
Nor for any outward part,
No, nor for my constant heart:
For those may fail or turn to ill,
So thou and I shall sever:
Keep therefore a true woman's eye,
And love me still, but know not why;
So hast thou the same reason still
To doat upon me ever.

1609 Edition

MATTHEW ARNOLD

2. The Forsaken Merman

Come, dear children, let us away;
Down and away below.
Now my brothers call from the bay;
Now the great winds shorewards blow;
Now the salt tides seawards flow;
Now the wild white horses play,
Champ and chafe and toss in the spray.
Children dear, let us away.
This way, this way.

Call her once before you go.
Call once yet.
In a voice that she will know:

"Margaret! Margaret!"
Children's voices should be dear
(Call once more) to a mother's ear:
Children's voices, wild with pain.
Surely she will come again.
Call her once and come away.
This way, this way.
"Mother dear, we cannot stay."
The wild white horses foam and fret.
Margaret! Margaret!

Come, dear children, come away down.
Call no more.
One last look at the white-wall'd town,
And the little grey church on the windy shore.
Then come down.
She will not come though you call all day.
Come away, come away.

Children dear, was it yesterday
We heard the sweet bells over the bay?
In the caverns where we lay,
Through the surf and through the swell,
The far-off sound of a silver bell?
Sand-strewn caverns, cool and deep,
Where the winds are all asleep;
Where the spent lights quiver and gleam;
Where the salt weed sways in the stream;
Where the sea-beasts rang'd all round
Feed in the ooze of their pasture-ground;
Where the sea-snakes coil and twine,
Dry their mail and bask in the brine;
Where great whales come sailing by,
Sail and sail, with unshut eye,
Round the world for ever and aye?
When did music come this way?
Children dear, was it yesterday?

Children dear, was it yesterday
(Call yet once) that she went away?
Once she sate with you and me,
On a red gold throne in the heart of the sea,
And the youngest sate on her knee.
She comb'd its bright hair, and she tended it well,
When down swung the sound of the far-off bell.
She sigh'd, she look'd up through the clear green sea.
She said; "I must go, for my kinsfolk pray
In the little grey church on the shore to-day.
'Twill be Easter-time in the world—ah me!
And I lose my poor soul, Merman, here with thee."
I said; "Go up, dear heart, through the waves.
Say thy prayer, and come back to the kind sea-caves."
She smil'd, she went up through the surf in the bay.
Children dear, was it yesterday?

Children dear, were we long alone?
"The sea grows stormy, the little ones moan.
Long prayers," I said, "in the world they say.
Come," I said, and we rose through the surf in the bay.
We went up the beach, by the sandy down
Where the sea-stocks bloom, to the white-wall'd town.
Through the narrow pav'd streets, where all was still,
To the little grey church on the windy hill.
From the church came a murmur of folk at their prayers,
But we stood without in the cold blowing airs.
We climb'd on the graves, on the stones, worn with rains,
And we gaz'd up the aisle through the small leaded panes.
She sate by the pillar; we saw her clear:
"Margaret, hist! come quick, we are here.
Dear heart," I said, "we are long alone.
The sea grows stormy, the little ones moan."
But, ah, she gave me never a look,
For her eyes were seal'd to the holy book.
"Loud prays the priest; shut stands the door."

Come away, children, call no more.
Come away, come down, call no more.

   Down, down, down.
   Down to the depths of the sea.
She sits at her wheel in the humming town,
     Singing most joyfully.
Hark, what she sings: "O joy, O joy,
For the humming street, and the child with its toy.
For the priest, and the bell, and the holy well.
   For the wheel where I spun,
   And the blessed light of the sun."
   And so she sings her fill,
   Singing most joyfully,
   Till the shuttle falls from her hand,
   And the whizzing wheel stands still.

She steals to the window, and looks at the sand;
   And over the sand at the sea;
   And her eyes are set in a stare;
   And anon there breaks a sigh,
   And anon there drops a tear,
   From a sorrow-clouded eye,
   And a heart sorrow-laden,
     A long, long sigh.
For the cold strange eyes of a little Mermaiden,
   And the gleam of her golden hair.

    Come away, away children.
Come children, come down.
The hoarse wind blows colder;
Lights shine in the town.
She will start from her slumber
When gusts shake the door;
She will hear the winds howling,
Will hear the waves roar.
We shall see, while above us

The waves roar and whirl,
A ceiling of amber,
A pavement of pearl.
Singing, "Here came a mortal,
But faithless was she.
And alone dwell for ever
The kings of the sea."

But, children, at midnight,
When soft the winds blow;
When clear falls the moonlight;
When spring-tides are low:
When sweet airs come seaward
From heaths starr'd with broom;
And high rocks throw mildly
On the blanch'd sands a gloom:
Up the still, glistening beaches,
Up the creeks we will hie;
Over banks of bright seaweed
The ebb-tide leaves dry.
We will gaze, from the sand-hills,
At the white, sleeping town;
At the church on the hill-side—

And then come back down.
Singing, "There dwells a lov'd one,
But cruel is she.
She left lonely for ever
The kings of the sea."

1857 Edition

ANNA LAETITIA BARBAULD

3. Life

Animula, vagula, blandula

Life! I know not what thou art,
But know that thou and I must part;
And when, or how, or where we met,
I own to me's a secret yet.
But this I know, when thou art fled,
Where'er they lay these limbs, this head,
No clod so valueless shall be,
As all that then remains of me.

O whither, whither dost thou fly,
Where bend unseen thy trackless course,
  And in this strange divorce,
Ah tell where I must seek this compound I?
To the vast ocean of empyreal flame,
  From whence thy essence came,
  Dost thou thy flight pursue, when freed
  From matter's base encumbering weed?
    Or dost thou, hid from sight,
    Wait, like some spell-bound knight,
Through blank oblivious years the appointed hour,
To break thy trance and reassume thy power?
Yet canst thou without thought or feeling be?
O say what art thou, when no more thou'rt thee?

Life! we've been long together,
Through pleasant and through cloudy weather;
  'Tis hard to part when friends are dear;
  Perhaps 'twill cost a sigh, a tear;
  Then steal away, give little warning,
    Choose thine own time;
Say not Good night, but in some brighter clime
    Bid me Good morning.

1825 Edition

ROBERT BROWNING

4. Song from "Pippa Passes"

The year's at the spring
And day's at the morn;
Morning's at seven;
The hill-side's dew-pearled;
The lark's on the wing;
The snail's on the thorn:
God's in his heaven—
All's right with the world!

5. Song from "Pippa Passes"

You'll love me yet!—and I can tarry
*   Your love's protracted growing:*
June reared that bunch of flowers you carry,
*   From seeds of April's sowing.*

I plant a heartful now: some seed
*   At least is sure to strike,*
And yield—what you'll not pluck indeed,
*   Not love, but, may be, like.*

You'll look at least on love's remains,
*   A grave's one violet:*
Your look?—that pays a thousand pains.
*   What's death? You'll love me yet!*

6. The Lost Mistress

I

All's over, then: does truth sound bitter
As one at first believes?
Hark, 'tis the sparrows' good-night twitter
About your cottage eaves!

II

And the leaf-buds on the vine are woolly,
I noticed that, to-day;
One day more bursts them open fully
—You know the red turns grey.

III

To-morrow we meet the same then, dearest?
May I take your hand in mine?
Mere friends are we,—well, friends the merest
Keep much that I resign:

IV

For each glance of the eye so bright and black,
Though I keep with heart's endeavour,—
Your voice, when you wish the snowdrops back,
Though it stay in my soul for ever!—

V

Yet I will but say what mere friends say,
Or only a thought stronger;
I will hold your hand but as long as all may,
Or so very little longer!

9

7. Home-Thoughts, from the Sea

Nobly, nobly Cape Saint Vincent to the North-west died away;
Sunset ran, one glorious blood-red, reeking into Cadiz Bay;
Bluish 'mid the burning water, full in face Trafalgar lay;
In the dimmest North-east distance dawned Gibraltar grand and grey;
"Here and here did England help me: how can I help England?"—say,
Whoso turns as I, this evening, turn to God to praise and pray,
While Jove's planet rises yonder, silent over Africa.

8. Epilogue

At the midnight in the silence of the sleep-time,
 When you set your fancies free,
Will they pass to where—by death, fools think, imprisoned—
Low he lies who once so loved you, whom you loved so,
  —Pity me?

Oh to love so, be so loved, yet so mistaken!
 What had I on earth to do
With the slothful, with the mawkish, the unmanly?
Like the aimless, helpless, hopeless, did I drivel
  —Being—who?

One who never turned his back but marched breast forward,
 Never doubted clouds would break,
Never dreamed, though right were worsted, wrong would triumph,
Held we fall to rise, are baffled to fight better,
  Sleep to wake.

No, at noonday in the bustle of man's work-time
 Greet the unseen with a cheer!
Bid him forward, breast and back as either should be,
"Strive and thrive!" cry "Speed,—fight on, fare ever
  There as here!"

                        1896 Edition

ROBERT BURNS

9. The Silver Tassie

I

Go, fetch to me a pint o' wine,
  And fill it in a silver tassie,
That I may drink before I go
  A service to my bonie lassie!
The boat rocks at the pier o' Leith,
  Fu' loud the wind blaws frae the Ferry,
The ship rides by the Berwick-Law,
  And I maun leave my bonie Mary.

II

The trumpets sound, the banners fly,
  The glittering spears are rankèd ready,
The shouts o' war are heard afar,
  The battle closes deep and bloody.
It's not the roar o' sea or shore
  Wad mak me langer wish to tarry,
Nor shouts o' war that's heard afar:
  It's leaving thee, my bonie Mary!

10. Of a' the Airts

I

Of a' the airts the wind can blaw
  I dearly like the west,
For there the bonie lassie lives,
  The lassie I lo'e best.
There wild woods grow, and rivers row,
  And monie a hill between,
But day and night my fancy's flight
  Is ever wi' my Jean.

I see her in the dewy flowers—
    I see her sweet and fair.
I hear her in the tunefu' birds—
    I hear her charm the air.
There's not a bonie flower that springs
    By fountain, shaw, or green,
There's not a bonie bird that sings,
    But minds me o' my Jean.

11. John Anderson my Jo

I

John Anderson my jo, John,
    When we were first acquent,
Your locks were like the raven,
    Your bonie brow was brent;
But now your brow is beld, John,
    Your locks are like the snaw,
But blessings on your frosty pow,
    John Anderson my jo!

II

John Anderson my jo, John,
    We clamb the hill thegither,
And monie a cantie day, John,
    We've had wi' ane anither;
Now we maun totter down, John,
    And hand in hand we'll go,
And sleep thegither at the foot,
    John Anderson my jo!

12. Ae Fond Kiss

I

Ae fond kiss, and then we sever!
Ae farewell, and then forever!
Deep in heart-wrung tears I'll pledge thee,
Warring sighs and groans I'll wage thee.
Who shall say that Fortune grieves him,
While the star of hope she leaves him?
Me, nae cheerfu' twinkle lights me,
Dark despair around benights me.

II

I'll ne'er blame my partial fancy:
Naething could resist my Nancy!
But to see her was to love her,
Love but her, and love for ever.
Had we never lov'd sae kindly,
Had we never lov'd sae blindly,
Never met—or never parted—
We had ne'er been broken-hearted.

III

Fare-thee-weel, thou first and fairest!
Fare-thee-weel, thou best and dearest!
Thine be ilka joy and treasure,
Peace, Enjoyment, Love, and Pleasure!
Ae fond kiss, and then we sever!
Ae farewell, alas, for ever!
Deep in heart-wrung tears I'll pledge thee,
Warring sighs and groans I'll wage thee.

13. Ye Flowery Banks

I

Ye flowery banks o' bonie Doon,
How can ye blume sae fair?
How can ye chant, ye little birds,
And I sae fu' o' care?

II

Thou'll break my heart, thou bonie bird,
That sings upon the bough:
Thou minds me o' the happy days
When my fause Luve was true!

III

Thou'll break my heart, thou bonie bird,
That sings beside thy mate:
For sae I sat, and sae I sang,
And wist na o' my fate!

IV

Aft hae I rov'd by bonie Doon
To see the woodbine twine,
And ilka bird sang o' its luve,
And sae did I o' mine.

V

Wi' lightsome heart I pu'd a rose
Frae aff its thorny tree,
And my fause luver staw my rose,
But left the thorn wi' me.

14. A Red, Red Rose

I

O, my luve is like a red, red rose,
That's newly sprung in June.
O, my luve is like the melodie,
That's sweetly play'd in tune.

II

As fair art thou, my bonie lass,
So deep in luve am I,
And I will luve thee still, my dear,
Till a' the seas gang dry.

III

Till a' the seas gang dry, my dear,
And the rocks melt wi' the sun!
And I will luve thee still, my dear,
While the sands o' life shall run.

IV

And fare the weel, my only luve,
And fare the weel a while!
And I will come again, my luve,
Tho' it were ten thousand mile!

15. Mary Morison

I

O Mary, at thy window be!
It is the wish'd, the trysted hour.
Those smiles and glances let me see,
That make the miser's treasure poor.
How blythely wad I bide the stoure,
A weary slave frae sun to sun,
Could I the rich reward secure—
The lovely Mary Morison!

II

Yestreen, when to the trembling string
The dance gaed thro' the lighted ha',
To thee my fancy took its wing,
I sat, but neither heard or saw:
Tho' this was fair, and that was braw,
And yon the toast of a' the town,
I sigh'd and said amang them a':—
"Ye are na Mary Morison!"

III

O Mary, canst thou wreck his peace
Wha for thy sake wad gladly die?
Or canst thou break that heart of his
Whase only faut is loving thee?
If love for love thou wilt na gie,
At least be pity to me shown:
A thought ungentle canna be
The thought o' Mary Morison.

Henderson and Henley's Text

16

LORD BYRON

16. She Walks in Beauty

I

She walks in Beauty, like the night
   Of cloudless climes and starry skies;
And all that's best of dark and bright
   Meet in her aspect and her eyes:
Thus mellowed to that tender light
   Which Heaven to gaudy day denies.

II

One shade the more, one ray the less,
   Had half impaired the nameless grace
Which waves in every raven tress,
   Or softly lightens o'er her face;
Where thoughts serenely sweet express,
   How pure, how dear their dwelling-place.

III

And on that cheek, and o'er that brow,
   So soft, so calm, yet eloquent,
The smiles that win, the tints that glow,
   But tell of days in goodness spent,
A mind at peace with all below,
   A heart whose love is innocent!

17. Oh! Snatched Away in Beauty's Bloom

I

Oh! snatched away in beauty's bloom,
On thee shall press no ponderous tomb;
But on thy turf shall roses rear
Their leaves, the earliest of the year;
And the wild cypress wave in tender gloom:

II

And oft by yon blue gushing stream
Shall Sorrow lean her drooping head,
And feed deep thought with many a dream,
And lingering pause and lightly tread;
Fond wretch! as if her step disturbed the dead!

III

Away! we know that tears are vain,
That Death nor heeds nor hears distress:
Will this unteach us to complain?
Or make one mourner weep the less?
And thou—who tell'st me to forget,
Thy looks are wan, thine eyes are wet.

18. Song from "The Corsair"

I

Deep in my soul that tender secret dwells,
    Lonely and lost to light for evermore,
Save when to thine my heart responsive swells,
    Then trembles into silence as before.

II

There, in its centre, a sepulchral lamp
    Burns the slow flame, eternal—but unseen;
Which not the darkness of Despair can damp,
    Though vain its ray as it had never been.

III

Remember me—Oh! pass not thou my grave
    Without one thought whose relics there recline:
The only pang my bosom dare not brave
    Must be to find forgetfulness in thine.

IV

My fondest—faintest—latest accents hear—
    Grief for the dead not Virtue can reprove;
Then give me all I ever asked—a tear,
    The first—last—sole reward of so much love!

19. Song from "Don Juan"

I

The Isles of Greece, the Isles of Greece!
    Where burning Sappho loved and sung,
Where grew the arts of War and Peace,
    Where Delos rose, and Phœbus sprung!
Eternal summer gilds them yet,
But all, except their Sun, is set.

II

The Scian and the Teian muse,
    The Hero's harp, the Lover's lute,
Have found the fame your shores refuse:
    Their place of birth alone is mute
To sounds which echo further west
Than your Sires' "Islands of the Blest."

III

The mountains look on Marathon—
    And Marathon looks on the sea;
And musing there an hour alone,
    I dreamed that Greece might still be free;
For standing on the Persians' grave,
I could not deem myself a slave.

IV

A King sate on the rocky brow
    Which looks o'er sea-born Salamis;
And ships, by thousands, lay below,
    And men in nations;—all were his!
He counted them at break of day—
And, when the Sun set, where were they?

V

And where are they? and where art thou,
    My Country? On thy voiceless shore
The heroic lay is tuneless now—

The heroic bosom beats no more!
    And must thy Lyre, so long divine,
Degenerate into hands like mine?

VI

'Tis something, in the dearth of Fame,
    Though linked among a fettered race,
To feel at least a patriot's shame,
    Even as I sing, suffuse my face;
For what is left the poet here?
For Greeks a blush—for Greece a tear.

VII

Must we but weep o'er days more blest?
    Must we but blush?—Our fathers bled.
Earth! render back from out thy breast
    A remnant of our Spartan dead!
Of the three hundred grant but three,
To make a new Thermopylae!

VIII

What, silent still? and silent all?
    Ah! no;—the voices of the dead
Sound like a distant torrent's fall,
    And answer, "Let one living head,
But one arise,—we come, we come!"
'Tis but the living who are dumb.

IX

In vain—in vain: strike other chords;
    Fill high the cup with Samian wine!
Leave battles to the Turkish hordes,
    And shed the blood of Scio's vine!
Hark! rising to the ignoble call—
How answers each bold Bacchanal!

X

You have the Pyrrhic dance as yet,

Where is the Pyrrhic phalanx gone?
Of two such lessons, why forget
　　The nobler and the manlier one?
You have the letters Cadmus gave—
Think ye he meant them for a slave?

XI

Fill high the bowl with Samian wine!
　　We will not think of themes like these!
It made Anacreon's song divine:
　　He served—but served Polycrates—
A Tyrant; but our masters then
Were still, at least, our countrymen.

XII

The Tyrant of the Chersonese
　　Was Freedom's best and bravest friend;
That tyrant was Miltiades!
　　Oh! that the present hour would lend
Another despot of the kind!
Such chains as his were sure to bind.

XIII

Fill high the bowl with Samian wine!
　　On Suli's rock, and Parga's shore,
Exists the remnant of a line
　　Such as the Doric mothers bore;
And there, perhaps, some seed is sown,
The Heracleidan blood might own.

XIV

Trust not for freedom to the Franks—
　　They have a king who buys and sells;
In native swords, and native ranks,
　　The only hope of courage dwells;
But Turkish force, and Latin fraud,
Would break your shield, however broad.

22

XV

Fill high the bowl with Samian wine!
Our virgins dance beneath the shade—
I see their glorious black eyes shine;
But gazing on each glowing maid,
My own the burning tear-drop laves,
To think such breasts must suckle slaves.

XVI

Place me on Sunium's marbled steep,
Where nothing, save the waves and I,
May hear our mutual murmurs sweep;
There, swan-like, let me sing and die:
A land of slaves shall ne'er be mine—
Dash down yon cup of Samian wine!

Coleridge's Text

THOMAS CAMPBELL

20. Hohenlinden

On Linden, when the sun was low,
All bloodless lay th' untrodden snow;
And dark as winter was the flow
Of Iser, rolling rapidly.

But Linden saw another sight,
When the drum beat, at dead of night,
Commanding fires of death to light
The darkness of her scenery.

By torch and trumpet fast array'd,
Each horseman drew his battle blade,
And furious every charger neigh'd,
To join the dreadful revelry.

Then shook the hills with thunder riv'n,
Then rush'd the steed to battle driv'n,
And louder than the bolts of heaven,
Far flash'd the red artillery.

But redder yet that light shall glow,
On Linden's hills of stained snow,
And bloodier yet the torrent flow
Of Iser, rolling rapidly.

'Tis morn, but scarce yon level sun
Can pierce the war-clouds, rolling dun,
Where furious Frank, and fiery Hun,
Shout in their sulph'rous canopy.

The combat deepens. On, ye brave,
Who rush to glory, or the grave!
Wave, Munich, all thy banners wave!

And charge with all thy chivalry!

Few, few, shall part where many meet!
The snow shall be their winding sheet,
And every turf beneath their feet,
Shall be a soldier's sepulchre.

1809 Edition

ARTHUR HUGH CLOUGH

21. Say not the Struggle Nought Availeth

Say not, the struggle nought availeth,
The labour and the wounds are vain,
The enemy faints not, nor faileth,
And as things have been they remain.

If hopes were dupes, fears may be liars;
It may be, in yon smoke concealed,
Your comrades chase e'en now the fliers,
And, but for you, possess the field.

For while the tired waves, vainly breaking,
Seem here no painful inch to gain,
Far back, through creeks and inlets making,
Comes silent, flooding in, the main.

And not by eastern windows only,
When daylight comes, comes in the light,
In front, the sun climbs slow, how slowly,
But westward, look, the land is bright.

1869 Edition

SAMUEL TAYLOR COLERIDGE

22. Youth and Age

Verse, a breeze mid blossoms straying,
Where Hope clung feeding, like a bee—
Both were mine! Life went a maying
 With Nature, Hope, and Poesy,
  When I was young!

When I was young?—Ah, woful when!
Ah! for the change 'twixt Now and Then!
This breathing house not built with hands,
This body that does me grievous wrong,
O'er aery cliffs and glittering sands,
How lightly then it flashed along:—
Like those trim skiffs, unknown of yore,
On winding lakes and rivers wide,
That ask no aid of sail or oar,
That fear no spite of wind or tide!
Nought cared this body for wind or weather
When Youth and I liv'd in't together.
Flowers are lovely; Love is flower-like;
Friendship is a sheltering tree;
O! the joys, that came down shower-like,
Of Friendship, Love, and Liberty,
  Ere I was old.

Ere I was old? Ah woful Ere,
Which tells me, Youth's no longer here!
O Youth! for years so many and sweet
'Tis known, that Thou and I were one,
I'll think it but a fond conceit—
It cannot be, that Thou art gone!
Thy vesper-bell hath not yet toll'd:—
And thou wert aye a masker bold!

What strange disguise hast now put on,
To make believe, that Thou art gone?
I see these locks in silvery slips,
This drooping gait, this altered size:
But springtide blossoms on thy lips,
And tears take sunshine from thine eyes!
Life is but thought: so think I will
That Youth and I are house-mates still.

Dew-drops are the gems of morning,
But the tears of mournful eve!
Where no hope is, life's a warning
That only serves to make us grieve,
              When we are old:

That only serves to make us grieve
With oft and tedious taking-leave,
Like some poor nigh-related guest,
That may not rudely be dismist.
Yet hath outstay'd his welcome while,
And tells the jest without the smile.

            1869 Edition

WILLIAM COLLINS

23. Written in the Year 1746

How sleep the brave, who sink to rest
By all their country's wishes bless'd!
When Spring, with dewy fingers cold,
Returns to deck their hallow'd mould,
She there shall dress a sweeter sod
Than Fancy's feet have ever trod.

By fairy hands their knell is rung;
By forms unseen their dirge is sung;
There Honour comes, a pilgrim gray,
To bless the turf that wraps their clay;
And Freedom shall a while repair,
To dwell a weeping hermit there.

1822 Edition

WILLIAM COWPER

24. To a Young Lady

Sweet stream that winds through yonder glade,
Apt emblem of a virtuous maid—
Silent and chaste she steals along,
Far from the world's gay busy throng,
With gentle, yet prevailing, force,
Intent upon her destin'd course;
Graceful and useful all she does,
Blessing and blest where'er she goes,
Pure-bosom'd as that wat'ry glass,
And heav'n reflected in her face.

1813 Edition

ALLAN CUNNINGHAM

25. A Wet Sheet and a Flowing Sea

A wet sheet and a flowing sea,
A wind that follows fast,
And fills the white and rustling sail,
And bends the gallant mast;
And bends the gallant mast, my boys,
While, like the eagle free,
Away the good ship flies, and leaves
Old England on the lee.

O for a soft and gentle wind!
I heard a fair one cry;
But give to me the snoring breeze,
And white waves heaving high;
And white waves heaving high, my boys,
The good ship tight and free—
The world of waters is our home,
And merry men are we.

There's tempest in yon horned moon,
And lightning in yon cloud;
And hark the music, mariners!
The wind is piping loud;
The wind is piping loud, my boys,
The lightning flashing free—
While the hollow oak our palace is,
Our heritage the sea.

1847 Edition

SIR WILLIAM DAVENANT

26. Song

The lark now leaves his wat'ry nest,
   And, climbing, shakes his dewy wings;
He takes this window for the east;
   And to implore your light, he sings:
"Awake, awake! the morn will never rise,
Till she can dress her beauty at your eyes.

"The merchant bows unto the seaman's star,
   The ploughman from the sun his season takes;
But still the lover wonders what they are,
   Who look for day before his mistress wakes.
Awake, awake! break thro' your veils of lawn!
Then draw your curtains, and begin the dawn."

1810 Edition

JOHN DRYDEN

27. A Song for St. Cecilia's Day, 1687

I

From harmony, from heav'nly harmony
   This universal frame began:
   When nature underneath a heap
      Of jarring atoms lay,
     And cou'd not heave her head,
The tuneful voice was heard from high,
     Arise, ye more than dead.
Then cold, and hot, and moist, and dry,
In order to their stations leap,

And Music's power obey.
From harmony, from heavenly harmony
   This universal frame began:
   From harmony to harmony
Through all the compass of the notes it ran,
The diapason closing full in Man.

II

What passion cannot Music raise and quell!
   When Jubal struck the corded shell,
His list'ning brethren stood around,
   And, wond'ring, on their faces fell
   To worship that celestial sound.
Less than a God they thought there could not dwell
   Within the hollow of that shell,
   That spoke so sweetly and so well.
What passion cannot Music raise and quell!

III

The trumpet's loud clangour
   Excites us to arms,
With shrill notes of anger
   And mortal alarms.
The double double double beat
   Of the thund'ring drum
Cries, Hark! the foes come;
Charge, charge, 'tis too late to retreat.

IV

   The soft complaining flute
   In dying notes discovers
   The woes of hopeless lovers,
Whose dirge is whisper'd by the warbling lute.

V

   Sharp violins proclaim
Their jealous pangs, and desperation,
Fury, frantic indignation,

Depth of pains, and height of passion,
For the fair, disdainful dame.

VI

But oh! what art can teach,
What human voice can reach,
The sacred organ's praise?
Notes inspiring holy love,
Notes that wing their heavenly ways
To mend the choirs above.

VII

Orpheus cou'd lead the savage race;
And trees uprooted left their place,
Sequacious of the lyre:
But bright Cecilia rais'd the wonder higher:
When to her organ vocal breath was giv'n,
An angel heard, and straight appear'd,
Mistaking Earth for Heav'n.

Grand Chorus

As from the pow'r of sacred lays
The spheres began to move,
And sung the great Creator's praise
To all the Bless'd above;
So when the last and dreadful hour
This crumbling pageant shall devour,
The trumpet shall be heard on high,
The dead shall live, the living die,
And Music shall untune the sky.

1743 Edition

OLIVER GOLDSMITH

28. Song

The wretch condemn'd with life to part,
Still, still on hope relies;
And ev'ry pang that rends the heart,
Bids expectation rise.

Hope, like the glimm'ring taper's light,
Adorns and cheers the way;
And still, as darker grows the night,
Emits a brighter ray.

1816 Edition

THOMAS GRAY

29. Elegy written in a Country Church-yard

The curfew tolls the knell of parting day,
The lowing herd winds slowly o'er the lea,
The ploughman homeward plods his weary way,
And leaves the world to darkness and to me.

Now fades the glimmering landscape on the sight,
And all the air a solemn stillness holds,
Save where the beetle wheels his droning flight,
And drowsy tinklings lull the distant folds:

Save that from yonder ivy-mantled tow'r,
The moping owl does to the moon complain
Of such as, wand'ring near her secret bow'r,
Molest her ancient solitary reign.

Beneath those rugged elms, that yew-tree's shade,

Where heaves the turf in many a mould'ring heap,
 Each in his narrow cell for ever laid,
  The rude forefathers of the hamlet sleep.

The breezy call of incense-breathing morn,
 The swallow twitt'ring from the straw-built shed,
The cock's shrill clarion, or the echoing horn,
 No more shall rouse them from their lowly bed.

For them no more the blazing hearth shall burn,
 Or busy housewife ply her evening care;
No children run to lisp their sire's return,
 Or climb his knees the envied kiss to share.

Oft did the harvest to their sickle yield,
 Their furrow oft the stubborn glebe has broke;
How jocund did they drive their team afield!
 How bow'd the woods beneath their sturdy stroke.

Let not ambition mock their useful toil,
 Their homely joys, and destiny obscure;
Nor grandeur hear with a disdainful smile
 The short and simple annals of the poor.

The boast of heraldry, the pomp of pow'r,
 And all that beauty, all that wealth e'er gave,
Await alike th'inevitable hour.
 The paths of glory lead but to the grave.

Nor you, ye proud, impute to these the fault,
 If memory o'er their tomb no trophies raise,
Where through the long-drawn aisle and fretted vault
 The pealing anthem swells the note of praise.

Can storied urn, or animated bust,
 Back to its mansion call the fleeting breath?
Can honour's voice provoke the silent dust,

Or flatt'ry soothe the dull cold ear of death?

Perhaps in this neglected spot is laid
Some heart once pregnant with celestial fire;
Hands, that the rod of empire might have sway'd,
Or wak'd to ecstasy the living lyre:

But knowledge to their eyes her ample page
Rich with the spoils of time did ne'er unroll;
Chill penury repress'd their noble rage,
And froze the genial current of the soul.

Full many a gem of purest ray serene
The dark unfathom'd caves of ocean bear:
Full many a flower is born to blush unseen,
And waste its sweetness on the desert air.

Some village-Hampden, that, with dauntless breast,
The little tyrant of his fields withstood,
Some mute inglorious Milton here may rest,
Some Cromwell guiltless of his country's blood.

Th' applause of list'ning senates to command,
The threats of pain and ruin to despise,
To scatter plenty o'er a smiling land,
And read their history in a nation's eyes,

Their lot forbade: nor circumscrib'd alone
Their growing virtues, but their crimes confin'd;
Forbade to wade thro' slaughter to a throne,
And shut the gates of mercy on mankind,

The struggling pangs of conscious truth to hide,
To quench the blushes of ingenuous shame,
Or heap the shrine of luxury and pride
With incense kindled at the Muse's flame.

Far from the madding crowd's ignoble strife,
  Their sober wishes never learn'd to stray;
Along the cool sequester'd vale of life
  They kept the noiseless tenour of their way.

Yet ev'n these bones from insult to protect
  Some frail memorial still erected nigh,
With uncouth rhymes and shapeless sculpture deck'd,
  Implores the passing tribute of a sigh.

Their name, their years, spelt by th' unletter'd Muse,
  The place of fame and elegy supply:
And many a holy text around she strews,
  That teach the rustic moralist to die.

For who, to dumb forgetfulness a prey,
  This pleasing anxious being e'er resign'd,
Left the warm precincts of the cheerful day,
  Nor cast one longing ling'ring look behind?

On some fond breast the parting soul relies,
  Some pious drops the closing eye requires;
E'en from the tomb the voice of nature cries,
  E'en in our ashes live their wonted fires.

For thee, who, mindful of th' unhonour'd dead,
  Dost in these lines their artless tale relate;
If chance, by lonely contemplation led,
  Some kindred spirit shall enquire thy fate,—

Haply some hoary-headed swain may say,
  'Oft have we seen him at the peep of dawn
Brushing with hasty steps the dews away,
  To meet the sun upon the upland lawn:

'There at the foot of yonder nodding beech,
  That wreathes its old fantastic roots so high,

36

His listless length at noontide would he stretch,
  And pore upon the brook that babbles by.

'Hard by yon wood, now smiling as in scorn,
  Mutt'ring his wayward fancies he would rove;
Now drooping, woful-wan, like one forlorn,
  Or craz'd with care, or cross'd in hopeless love.

'One morn I miss'd him on the custom'd hill,
  Along the heath, and near his fav'rite tree;
Another came; nor yet beside the rill,
  Nor up the lawn, nor at the wood was he:

'The next, with dirges due in sad array
  Slow through the church-way path we saw him borne:—
Approach and read (for thou canst read) the lay
  Grav'd on the stone beneath yon aged thorn.'

The Epitaph

Here rests his head upon the lap of earth
  A youth, to fortune and to fame unknown:
Fair science frown'd not on his humble birth,
  And melancholy mark'd him for her own.

Large was his bounty, and his soul sincere,
  Heaven did a recompense as largely send:
He gave to mis'ry (all he had) a tear,
  He gain'd from heav'n ('twas all he wish'd) a friend.

No farther seek his merits to disclose,
  Or draw his frailties from their dread abode,
(There they alike in trembling hope repose,)
  The bosom of his Father and his God.

                    Mitford's Text

37

WILLIAM ERNEST HENLEY

30. To R. T. H. B.

Out of the night that covers me,
  Black as the Pit from pole to pole,
I thank whatever gods may be
  For my unconquerable soul.

In the fell clutch of circumstance
  I have not winced nor cried aloud.
Under the bludgeonings of chance
  My head is bloody, but unbowed.

Beyond this place of wrath and tears
  Looms but the Horror of the shade,
And yet the menace of the years
  Finds, and shall find, me unafraid.

It matters not how strait the gate,
  How charged with punishments the scroll,
I am the master of my fate:
  I am the captain of my soul.

31. I. M.

Margaritae Sorori

(1886)

A late lark twitters from the quiet skies;
And from the west,
Where the sun, his day's work ended,
Lingers as in content,
There falls on the old, grey city
An influence luminous and serene,
A shining peace.

The smoke ascends
In a rosy-and-golden haze. The spires
Shine, and are changed. In the valley
Shadows rise. The lark sings on. The sun,
Closing his benediction,
Sinks, and the darkening air
Thrills with a sense of the triumphing night—
Night with her train of stars
And her great gift of sleep.
So be my passing!
My task accomplished and the long day done,
My wages taken, and in my heart
Some late lark singing,
Let me be gathered to the quiet west,
The sundown splendid and serene,
Death.

1898 Edition

GEORGE HERBERT

32. Virtue

Sweet day, so cool, so calm, so bright,
The bridal of the earth and sky:
The dew shall weep thy fall to-night;
　　For thou must die.

Sweet rose, whose hue angry and brave
Bids the rash gazer wipe his eye:
Thy root is ever in its grave,
　　And thou must die.

Sweet spring, full of sweet days and roses,
A box where sweets compacted lie;
My music shows ye have your closes,
　　And all must die.

Only a sweet and virtuous soul,
Like season'd timber, never gives;
But though the whole world turn to coal,
　　Then chiefly lives.

1633 Edition

ROBERT HERRICK

33. To the Virgins, to make much of Time

1. Gather ye rosebuds while ye may,
*   Old Time is still a-flying:*
And this same flower that smiles to-day,
*   To-morrow will be dying.*

2. The glorious lamp of heaven, the sun,
*   The higher he's a-getting;*
The sooner will his race be run,
*   And nearer he's to setting.*

3. That age is best, which is the first,
*   When youth and blood are warmer;*
But being spent, the worse, and worst
*   Times, still succeed the former.*

4. Then be not coy, but use your time;
*   And while ye may, go marry:*
For having lost but once your prime,
*   You may for ever tarry.*

34. To Anthea, who may command him anything.

1. Bid me to live, and I will live
    Thy Protestant to be:
Or bid me love, and I will give
    A loving heart to thee.

2. A heart as soft, a heart as kind,
    A heart as sound and free,
As in the whole world thou canst find,
    That heart I'll give to thee.

3. Bid that heart stay, and it will stay,
    To honour thy decree:
Or bid it languish quite away,
    And't shall do so for thee.

4. Bid me to weep, and I will weep,
    While I have eyes to see:
And having none, yet I will keep
    A heart to weep for thee.

5. Bid me despair, and I'll despair,
    Under that cypress tree:
Or bid me die, and I will dare
    E'en death, to die for thee.

6. Thou art my life, my love, my heart,
    The very eyes of me:
And hast command of every part,
    To live and die for thee.

Grosart's Text

THOMAS HOOD

35. The Death Bed

We watch'd her breathing through the night,
*   Her breathing soft and low,*
As in her breast the wave of life
*   Kept heaving to and fro.*

So silently we seem'd to speak,
*   So slowly moved about,*
As we had lent her half our powers
*   To eke her living out.*

Our very hopes belied our fears,
*   Our fears our hopes belied—*
We thought her dying when she slept,
*   And sleeping when she died.*

For when the morn came dim and sad,
*   And chill with early showers,*
Her quiet eyelids closed—she had
*   Another morn than ours.*

36. The Bridge of Sighs

"Drown'd! drown'd!"—Hamlet

One more Unfortunate,
Weary of breath,
Rashly importunate,
Gone to her death!

Take her up tenderly,
Lift her with care;

43

Fashion'd so slenderly,
Young, and so fair!

Look at her garments
Clinging like cerements;
Whilst the wave constantly
Drips from her clothing;
Take her up instantly,
Loving, not loathing.—

Touch her not scornfully;
Think of her mournfully,
Gently and humanly;
Not of the stains of her,
All that remains of her
Now is pure womanly.

Make no deep scrutiny
Into her mutiny
Rash and undutiful:
Past all dishonour,
Death has left on her
Only the beautiful.

Still, for all slips of hers,
One of Eve's family—
Wipe those poor lips of hers
Oozing so clammily.

Loop up her tresses
Escaped from the comb,
Her fair auburn tresses;
Whilst wonderment guesses
Where was her home?

Who was her father?
Who was her mother?

44

Had she a sister?
Had she a brother?
Or was there a dearer one
Still, and a nearer one
Yet, than all other?

Alas! for the rarity
Of Christian charity
Under the sun!
Oh! it was pitiful!
Near a whole city full,
Home she had none.

Sisterly, brotherly,
Fatherly, motherly
Feelings had changed:
Love, by harsh evidence,
Thrown from its eminence;
Even God's providence
Seeming estranged.

Where the lamps quiver
So far in the river,
With many a light
From window and casement,
From garret to basement,
She stood, with amazement,
Houseless by night.

The bleak wind of March
Made her tremble and shiver;
But not the dark arch,
Or the black flowing river:
Mad from life's history,
Glad to death's mystery,
Swift to be hurl'd—
Any where, any where

Out of the world!

In she plunged boldly,
No matter how coldly
The rough river ran,—
Over the brink of it,
Picture it—think of it,
Dissolute Man!
Lave in it, drink of it,
Then, if you can!

Take her up tenderly,
Lift her with care;
Fashion'd so slenderly,
Young, and so fair!

Ere her limbs frigidly
Stiffen too rigidly,
Decently,—kindly,—
Smooth, and compose them;
And her eyes, close them,
Staring so blindly!

Dreadfully staring
Thro' muddy impurity,
As when with the daring
Last look of despairing
Fix'd on futurity.

Perishing gloomily,
Spurr'd by contumely,
Cold inhumanity,
Burning insanity,
Into her rest.—
Cross her hands humbly,
As if praying dumbly,
Over her breast!

Owning her weakness,
Her evil behaviour,
And leaving, with meekness,
Her sins to her Saviour!

37. I Remember, I Remember

I remember, I remember,
The house where I was born,
The little window where the sun
Came peeping in at morn;
He never came a wink too soon,
Nor brought too long a day,
But now, I often wish the night
Had borne my breath away!

I remember, I remember,
The roses, red and white,
The violets, and the lily cups,
Those flowers made of light!
The lilacs where the robin built,
And where my brother set
The laburnum on his birth-day,—
The tree is living yet!

I remember, I remember
Where I was used to swing,
And thought the air must rush as fresh
To swallows on the wing;
My spirit flew in feathers then,
That is so heavy now,
And summer pools could hardly cool
The fever on my brow!

I remember, I remember
The fir trees dark and high;
I used to think their slender tops

Were close against the sky:
It was a childish ignorance,
But now 'tis little joy
To know I'm farther off from Heav'n
Than when I was a boy.

1862-3 Edition

BEN JONSON

38. To Celia

Drink to me, only with thine eyes,
  And I will pledge with mine;
Or leave a kiss but in the cup,
  And I'll not look for wine.
The thirst, that from the soul doth rise,
  Doth ask a drink divine:
But might I of Jove's nectar sup,
  I would not change for thine.

I sent thee late a rosy wreath,
  Not so much honouring thee,
As giving it a hope, that there
  It could not wither'd be.
But thou thereon didst only breathe,
  And sent'st it back to me:
Since when it grows, and smells, I swear,
  Not of itself, but thee.

Cunningham's Text

48

JOHN KEATS

39. On first looking into Chapman's Homer

Much have I travell'd in the realms of gold,
And many goodly states and kingdoms seen;
Round many western islands have I been
Which bards in fealty to Apollo hold.
Oft of one wide expanse had I been told
That deep-brow'd Homer rul'd as his demesne;
Yet did I never breathe its pure serene
Till I heard Chapman speak out loud and bold:
Then felt I like some watcher of the skies
When a new planet swims into his ken;
Or like stout Cortez when with eagle eyes
He star'd at the Pacific—and all his men
Looked at each other with a wild surmise—
Silent, upon a peak in Darien.

40. Ode to a Nightingale

1

My heart aches, and a drowsy numbness pains
My sense, as though of hemlock I had drunk,
Or emptied some dull opiate to the drains
One minute past, and Lethe-wards had sunk:
'Tis not through envy of thy happy lot,
But being too happy in thine happiness,—
That thou, light-winged Dryad of the trees,
In some melodious plot
Of beechen green, and shadows numberless,
Singest of summer in full-throated ease.

2

O for a draught of vintage! that hath been

49

Cool'd a long age in the deep-delved earth,
Tasting of Flora and the country green,
   Dance, and Provençal song, and sunburnt mirth!
O for a beaker full of the warm South,
   Full of the true, the blushful Hippocrene,
      With beaded bubbles winking at the brim,
         And purple-stained mouth;
That I might drink, and leave the world unseen,
      And with thee fade away into the forest dim:

3

Fade far away, dissolve, and quite forget
   What thou among the leaves hast never known,
The weariness, the fever, and the fret
   Here, where men sit and hear each other groan;
Where palsy shakes a few, sad, last gray hairs,
   Where youth grows pale, and spectre-thin, and dies;
      Where but to think is to be full of sorrow
        And leaden-ey'd despairs,
Where Beauty cannot keep her lustrous eyes,
      Or new Love pine at them beyond to-morrow.

4

Away! away! for I will fly to thee,
   Not charioted by Bacchus and his pards,
But on the viewless wings of Poesy,
   Though the dull brain perplexes and retards:
Already with thee! tender is the night,
   And haply the Queen-Moon is on her throne,
      Cluster'd around by all her starry Fays;
        But here there is no light,
Save what from heaven is with the breezes blown
      Through verdurous glooms and winding mossy ways.

5

I cannot see what flowers are at my feet,
   Nor what soft incense hangs upon the boughs,
But, in embalmed darkness, guess each sweet

Wherewith the seasonable month endows
The grass, the thicket, and the fruit-tree wild;
White hawthorn, and the pastoral eglantine;
Fast fading violets cover'd up in leaves;
And mid-May's eldest child,
The coming musk-rose, full of dewy wine,
The murmurous haunt of flies on summer eves.

6

Darkling I listen; and, for many a time
I have been half in love with easeful Death,
Call'd him soft names in many a mused rhyme,
To take into the air my quiet breath;
Now more than ever seems it rich to die,
To cease upon the midnight with no pain,
While thou art pouring forth thy soul abroad
In such an ecstasy!
Still wouldst thou sing, and I have ears in vain—
To thy high requiem become a sod.

7

Thou wast not born for death, immortal Bird!
No hungry generations tread thee down;
The voice I hear this passing night was heard
In ancient days by emperor and clown:
Perhaps the self-same song that found a path
Through the sad heart of Ruth, when, sick for home,
She stood in tears amid the alien corn;
The same that oft-times hath
Charm'd magic casements, opening on the foam
Of perilous seas, in faery lands forlorn.

8

Forlorn! the very word is like a bell
To toll me back from thee to my sole self!
Adieu! the fancy cannot cheat so well
As she is fam'd to do, deceiving elf.
Adieu! adieu! thy plaintive anthem fades

Past the near meadows, over the still stream,
    Up the hill-side; and now 'tis buried deep
       In the next valley-glades:
Was it a vision, or a waking dream?
    Fled is that music:—do I wake or sleep?

41. Ode on a Grecian Urn

1

Thou still unravish'd bride of quietness,
    Thou foster-child of silence and slow time,
Sylvan historian, who canst thus express
    A flowery tale more sweetly than our rhyme:
What leaf-fring'd legend haunts about thy shape
    Of deities or mortals, or of both,
       In Tempe or the dales of Arcady?
    What men or gods are these? What maidens loth?
What mad pursuit? What struggle to escape?
       What pipes and timbrels? What wild ecstasy?

2

Heard melodies are sweet, but those unheard
    Are sweeter; therefore, ye soft pipes, play on;
Not to the sensual ear, but, more endear'd,
    Pipe to the spirit ditties of no tone:
Fair youth, beneath the trees, thou canst not leave
    Thy song, nor ever can those trees be bare;
       Bold Lover, never, never canst thou kiss,
    Though winning near the goal—yet, do not grieve;
She cannot fade, though thou hast not thy bliss,
       For ever wilt thou love, and she be fair!

3

Ah, happy, happy boughs! that cannot shed
    Your leaves, nor ever bid the Spring adieu;
And, happy melodist, unwearied,

For ever piping songs for ever new;
More happy love! more happy, happy love!
For ever warm and still to be enjoy'd,
For ever panting, and for ever young;
All breathing human passion far above,
That leaves a heart high-sorrowful and cloy'd,
A burning forehead, and a parching tongue.

4

Who are these coming to the sacrifice?
To what green altar, O mysterious priest,
Lead'st thou that heifer lowing at the skies,
And all her silken flanks with garlands drest?
What little town by river or sea shore,
Or mountain-built with peaceful citadel,
Is emptied of this folk, this pious morn?
And, little town, thy streets for evermore
Will silent be; and not a soul to tell
Why thou art desolate, can e'er return.

5

O Attic shape! Fair attitude! with brede
Of marble men and maidens overwrought,
With forest branches and the trodden weed;
Thou, silent form, dost tease us out of thought
As doth eternity: Cold Pastoral!
When old age shall this generation waste,
Thou shalt remain, in midst of other woe
Than ours, a friend to man, to whom thou say'st,
'Beauty is truth, truth beauty,'—that is all
Ye know on earth, and all ye need to know.

53

42. To Autumn

1

Season of mists and mellow fruitfulness,
   Close bosom-friend of the maturing sun;
Conspiring with him how to load and bless
   With fruit the vines that round the thatch-eves run;
To bend with apples the moss'd cottage-trees,
   And fill all fruit with ripeness to the core;
      To swell the gourd, and plump the hazel shells
With a sweet kernel; to set budding more,
And still more, later flowers for the bees,
Until they think warm days will never cease,
      For Summer has o'er-brimm'd their clammy cells.

2

Who hath not seen thee oft amid thy store?
   Sometimes whoever seeks abroad may find
Thee sitting careless on a granary floor,
   Thy hair soft-lifted by the winnowing wind;
Or on a half-reap'd furrow sound asleep,
   Drows'd with the fume of poppies, while thy hook
      Spares the next swath and all its twined flowers:
And sometimes like a gleaner thou dost keep
Steady thy laden head across a brook;
Or by a cyder-press, with patient look,
      Thou watchest the last oozings hours by hours.

3

Where are the songs of Spring? Ay, where are they?
   Think not of them, thou hast thy music too, —
While barred clouds bloom the soft-dying day, —
   And touch the stubble-plains with rosy hue;
Then in a wailful choir the small gnats mourn
   Among the river sallows, borne aloft
      Or sinking as the light wind lives or dies;
And full-grown lambs loud bleat from hilly bourn;

Hedge-crickets sing; and now with treble soft
The red-breast whistles from a garden-croft;
    And gathering swallows twitter in the skies.

43. Ode on Melancholy

1

No, no, go not to Lethe, neither twist
    Wolf's-bane, tight-rooted, for its poisonous wine;
Nor suffer thy pale forehead to be kiss'd
    By nightshade, ruby grape of Proserpine;
Make not your rosary of yew-berries,
    Nor let the beetle, nor the death-moth be
        Your mournful Psyche, nor the downy owl
A partner in your sorrow's mysteries;
    For shade to shade will come too drowsily,
        And drown the wakeful anguish of the soul.

2

But when the melancholy fit shall fall
    Sudden from heaven like a weeping cloud,
That fosters the droop-headed flowers all,
    And hides the green hill in an April shroud;
Then glut thy sorrow on a morning rose,
    Or on the rainbow of the salt sand-wave,
        Or on the wealth of globed peonies;
Or if thy mistress some rich anger shows,
    Emprison her soft hand, and let her rave,
        And feed deep, deep upon her peerless eyes.

3

She dwells with Beauty—Beauty that must die;
    And Joy, whose hand is ever at his lips
Bidding adieu; and aching Pleasure nigh,
    Turning to poison while the bee-mouth sips:
Ay, in the very temple of Delight

> Veil'd Melancholy has her sovran shrine,
>> Though seen of none save him whose strenuous tongue
> Can burst Joy's grape against his palate fine;
>> His soul shall taste the sadness of her might,
>> And be among her cloudy trophies hung.

44. La Belle Dame sans Merci

1

Ah, what can ail thee, wretched wight,
Alone and palely loitering;
The sedge is wither'd from the lake,
And no birds sing.

2

Ah, what can ail thee, wretched wight,
So haggard and so woe-begone?
The squirrel's granary is full,
And the harvest's done.

3

I see a lily on thy brow,
With anguish moist and fever dew;
And on thy cheek a fading rose
Fast withereth too.

4

I met a lady in the meads
Full beautiful, a faery's child;
Her hair was long, her foot was light,
And her eyes were wild.

5

I set her on my pacing steed,
And nothing else saw all day long;
For sideways would she lean, and sing
A faery's song.

6

I made a garland for her head,
  And bracelets too, and fragrant zone;
She look'd at me as she did love,
  And made sweet moan.

7

She found me roots of relish sweet,
  And honey wild, and manna dew;
And sure in language strange she said,
  I love thee true.

8

She took me to her elfin grot,
  And there she gaz'd and sighed deep,
And there I shut her wild sad eyes—
  So kiss'd to sleep.

9

And there we slumber'd on the moss,
  And there I dream'd, ah woe betide,
The latest dream I ever dream'd
  On the cold hill-side.

10

I saw pale kings, and princes too,
  Pale warriors, death-pale were they all;
Who cry'd—"La belle Dame sans merci
  Hath thee in thrall!"

11

I saw their starv'd lips in the gloam
With horrid warning gaped wide,
And I awoke, and found me here
On the cold hill-side.

12

And this is why I sojourn here

Alone and palely loitering,
Though the sedge is wither'd from the lake,
And no birds sing.

45. Sonnet

When I have fears that I may cease to be
*   Before my pen has glean'd my teeming brain,*
Before high-piled books, in charactery,
*   Hold like rich garners the full ripen'd grain;*
When I behold, upon the night's starr'd face,
*   Huge cloudy symbols of a high romance,*
And think that I may never live to trace
*   Their shadows, with the magic hand of chance;*
And when I feel, fair creature of an hour,
*   That I shall never look upon thee more,*
Never have relish in the faery power
*   Of unreflecting love;—then on the shore*
Of the wide world I stand alone, and think
Till love and fame to nothingness do sink.

Buxton Forman's Text

CHARLES LAMB

46. The Old Familiar Faces

Where are they gone, the old familiar faces?
I had a mother, but she died, and left me,
Died prematurely in a day of horrors—
All, all are gone, the old familiar faces.

I have had playmates, I have had companions,
In my days of childhood, in my joyful school days—
All, all are gone, the old familiar faces.

I have been laughing, I have been carousing,
Drinking late, sitting late, with my bosom cronies—
All, all are gone, the old familiar faces.

I lov'd a love once, fairest among women;
Clos'd are her doors on me, I must not see her—
All, all are gone, the old familiar faces.

I have a friend, a kinder friend has no man.
Like an ingrate, I left my friend abruptly;
Left him, to muse on the old familiar faces.

Ghost-like, I pac'd round the haunts of my childhood.
Earth seem'd a desert I was bound to traverse,
Seeking to find the old familiar faces.

Friend of my bosom, thou more than a brother!
Why were not thou born in my father's dwelling?
So might we talk of the old familiar faces.

For some they have died, and some they have left me,
And some are taken from me; all are departed;
All, all are gone, the old familiar faces.
1798 Edition

WALTER SAVAGE LANDOR

47. The Maid's Lament

I loved him not; and yet now he is gone
    I feel I am alone.
I check'd him while he spoke; yet could he speak,
    Alas! I would not check.
For reasons not to love him once I sought,
    And wearied all my thought
To vex myself and him: I now would give
    My love, could he but live
Who lately lived for me, and when he found
    'Twas vain, in holy ground
He hid his face amid the shades of death.
    I waste for him my breath
Who wasted his for me: but mine returns,
    And this lorn bosom burns
With stifling heat, heaving it up in sleep,
    And waking me to weep
Tears that had melted his soft heart: for years
    Wept he as bitter tears.
Merciful God! such was his latest prayer,
    These may she never share!
Quieter is his breath, his breast more cold,
    Than daisies in the mould,
Where children spell, athwart the churchyard gate,
    His name and life's brief date.
Pray for him, gentle souls, whoe'er you be,
    And oh! pray too for me!

1868 Edition

RICHARD LOVELACE

48. To Lucasta. Going to the Wars

Tell me not, (sweet,) I am unkind,
  That from the nunnery
Of thy chaste breast and quiet mind
  To war and arms I fly.

True: a new Mistress now I chase,
  The first foe in the field;
And with a stronger faith embrace
  A sword, a horse, a shield.

Yet this inconstancy is such,
  As you too shall adore;
I could not love thee, dear, so much,
  Lov'd I not Honour more.

Carew Hazlitt's Text

JOHN MILTON

49. On the Morning of Christ's Nativity

I

This is the month, and this the happy morn,
  Wherein the Son of Heaven's eternal King,
Of wedded Maid and Virgin-Mother born,
  Our great redemption from above did bring;
  For so the holy sages once did sing,
That he our deadly forfeit should release,
And with his Father work us a perpetual peace.

61

II

That glorious form, that light unsufferable,
  And that far-beaming blaze of majesty,
Wherewith he wont at Heaven's high council-table
  To sit the midst of Trinal Unity,
    He laid aside; and, here with us to be,
  Forsook the courts of everlasting day,
And chose with us a darksome house of mortal clay.

III

Say, heavenly Muse, shall not thy sacred vein
  Afford a present to the Infant God?
Hast thou no verse, no hymn, or solemn strain,
  To welcome him to this his new abode,
    Now, while the heaven, by the Sun's team untrod,
  Hath took no print of the approaching light,
And all the spangled host keep watch in squadrons bright?

IV

See how from far upon the eastern road
  The star-led wizards haste with odours sweet!
Oh! run, prevent them with thy humble ode,
  And lay it lowly at his blessed feet;
    Have thou the honour first thy Lord to greet,
  And join thy voice unto the angel quire,
From out his secret altar touched with hallowed fire.

The Hymn

I

It was the winter wild,
While the heaven-born child
All meanly wrapt in the rude manger lies;
  Nature in awe to him
  Had doffed her gaudy trim,
With her great Master so to sympathize.
  It was no season then for her

62

To wanton with the Sun her lusty paramour.

II

Only with speeches fair
She woos the gentle air
To hide her guilty front with innocent snow,
And on her naked shame,
Pollute with sinful blame,
The saintly veil of maiden-white to throw,
Confounded, that her Maker's eyes
Should look so near upon her foul deformities.

III

But he, her fears to cease,
Sent down the meek-eyed Peace;
She, crowned with olive-green, came softly sliding
Down through the turning sphere,
His ready harbinger,
With turtle wing the amorous clouds dividing;
And, waving wide her myrtle wand,
She strikes an universal peace through sea and land.

IV

No war or battle's sound
Was heard the world around;
The idle spear and shield were high up hung;
The hooked chariot stood,
Unstained with hostile blood;
The trumpet spake not to the armed throng;
And kings sat still with awful eye,
As if they surely knew their sovran Lord was by.

V

But peaceful was the night,
Wherein the Prince of Light
His reign of peace upon the earth began.
The winds, with wonder whist,
Smoothly the waters kissed,

Whispering new joys to the mild ocean,
Who now hath quite forgot to rave,
While birds of calm sit brooding on the charmed wave.

VI

The stars, with deep amaze,
Stand fixed in steadfast gaze,
Bending one way their precious influence,
And will not take their flight,
For all the morning-light,
Or Lucifer that often warned them thence;
But in their glimmering orbs did glow,
Until their Lord himself bespake, and bid them go.

VII

And, though the shady gloom
Had given day her room,
The sun himself withheld his wonted speed;
And hid his head for shame,
As his inferior flame
The new-enlightened world no more should need;
He saw a greater sun appear
Than his bright throne or burning axletree could bear.

VIII

The shepherds on the lawn,
Or ere the point of dawn,
Sat simply chatting in a rustic row;
Full little thought they than
That the mighty Pan
Was kindly come to live with them below.
Perhaps their loves, or else their sheep,
Was all that did their silly thoughts so busy keep.

IX

When such music sweet
Their hearts and ears did greet,
As never was by mortal finger strook;

Divinely-warbled voice
Answering the stringed noise,
As all their souls in blissful rapture took.
The air, such pleasure loth to lose,
With thousand echoes still prolongs each heavenly close.

X

Nature, that heard such sound,
Beneath the hollow round
Of Cynthia's seat, the airy region thrilling,
Now was almost won
To think her part was done,
And that her reign had here its last fulfilling.
She knew such harmony alone
Could hold all Heaven and Earth in happier union.

XI

At last surrounds their sight
A globe of circular light,
That with long beams the shame-faced Night arrayed.
The helmed Cherubim,
And sworded Seraphim,
Are seen, in glittering ranks with wings displayed,
Harping, in loud and solemn quire,
With unexpressive notes to Heaven's new-born Heir.

XII

Such music—as 'tis said—
Before was never made,
But when of old the Sons of Morning sung;
While the Creator great
His constellations set,
And the well-balanced World on hinges hung,
And cast the dark foundations deep,
And bid the weltering waves their oozy channel keep.

XIII

Ring out, ye crystal spheres!

Once bless our human ears,
—If ye have power to touch our senses so—
And let your silver-chime
Move in melodious time,
And let the base of heaven's deep organ blow;
And with your ninefold harmony
Make up full consort to the angelic symphony.

XIV

For if such holy song
Enwrap our fancy long,
Time will run back, and fetch the Age of Gold;
And speckled Vanity
Will sicken soon and die,
And leprous Sin will melt from earthly mould;
And Hell itself will pass away,
And leave her dolorous mansions to the peering day.

XV

Yea Truth and Justice then
Will down return to men,
Orbed in a rainbow, and like glories wearing;
Mercy will sit between,
Throned in celestial sheen,
With radiant feet the tissued clouds down steering;
And Heaven, as at some festival,
Will open wide the gates of her high palace-hall.

XVI

But wisest Fate says No,
This must not yet be so,
The Babe lies yet in smiling infancy,
That, on the bitter cross,
Must redeem our loss;
So both himself and us to glorify:
Yet first, to those ychained in sleep,
The wakeful trump of doom must thunder through the deep.

XVII

With such a horrid clang
As on Mount Sinai rang,
While the red fire and smouldering clouds outbrake,
The aged earth aghast,
With terror of that blast,
Shall from the surface to the centre shake;
When, at the world's last session,
The dreadful Judge in middle air shall spread his throne.

XVIII

And then at last our bliss
Full and perfect is,
But now begins; for from this happy day
The Old Dragon under ground,
In straiter limits bound,
Not half so far casts his usurped sway,
And, wroth to see his kingdom fail,
Swinges the scaly horror of his folded tail.

XIX

The oracles are dumb,
No voice or hideous hum
Runs through the arched roof in words deceiving.
Apollo from his shrine
Can no more divine,
With hollow shriek the steep of Delphos leaving.
No nightly trance, or breathed spell,
Inspires the pale-eyed priest from the prophetic cell.

XX

The lonely mountains o'er,
And the resounding shore,
A voice of weeping heard and loud lament;
From haunted spring, and dale
Edged with poplar pale,
The parting Genius is with sighing sent;

With flower-inwoven tresses torn
The Nymphs in twilight shade of tangled thickets mourn.

XXI

In consecrated earth,
And on the holy hearth,
The Lars and Lemures moan with midnight plaint;
In urns and altars round,
A drear and dying sound
Affrights the Flamens at their service quaint;
And the chill marble seems to sweat,
While each peculiar power forgoes his wonted seat.

XXII

Peor and Baälim
Forsake their temples dim,
With that twice battered god of Palestine;
And mooned Ashtaroth,
Heaven's queen and mother both,
Now sits not girt with tapers' holy shine;
The Lybic Hammon shrinks his horn;
In vain the Tyrian maids their wounded Thammuz mourn.

XXIII

And sullen Moloch, fled,
Hath left in shadows dread
His burning idol all of blackest hue;
In vain with cymbals' ring
They call the grisly king,
In dismal dance about the furnace blue;
The brutish gods of Nile as fast,
Isis, and Orus, and the dog Anubis haste.

XXIV

Nor is Osiris seen
In Memphian grove or green,
Trampling the unshowered grass with lowings loud;
Nor can he be at rest

Within his sacred chest,
Nought but profoundest hell can be his shroud;
In vain, with timbrelled anthems dark,
The sable-stoled sorcerers bear his worshipped ark.

XXV

He feels, from Juda's land,
The dreaded Infant's hand,
The rays of Bethlehem blind his dusky eyn;
Nor all the gods beside
Longer dare abide,
Nor Typhon huge ending in snaky twine.
Our Babe, to shew his Godhead true,
Can in his swaddling-bands control the damned crew.

XXVI

So when the sun in bed,
Curtained with cloudy red,
Pillows his chin upon an orient wave,
The flocking shadows pale
Troop to the infernal jail,
Each fettered ghost slips to his several grave,
And the yellow-skirted fayes
Fly after the Night steeds, leaving their moon-loved maze.

XXVII

But see! the Virgin blest
Hath laid her Babe to rest,
Time is our tedious song should here have ending;
Heaven's youngest-teemed star
Hath fixed her polished car,
Her sleeping Lord with handmaid-lamp attending;
And all about the courtly stable
Bright-harnessed angels sit in order serviceable.

50. L'Allegro

Hence, loathed Melancholy!
Of Cerberus and blackest Midnight born,
In Stygian cave forlorn,
'Mongst horrid shapes, and shrieks, and sights unholy.
Find out some uncouth cell,
Where brooding Darkness spreads his jealous wings,
And the night-raven sings;
There, under ebon shades and low-browed rocks
As ragged as thy locks,
In dark Cimmerian desert ever dwell.
But come, thou Goddess fair and free,
In Heaven yclept Euphrosynè,
And by men, heart-easing Mirth;
Whom lovely Venus, at a birth
With two sister Graces more,
To ivy-crowned Bacchus bore;
Or whether, as some sager sing,
The frolic wind that breathes the spring,
Zephyr, with Aurora playing,
As he met her once a-maying,
There, on beds of violets blue,
And fresh-blown roses washed in dew,
Filled her with thee, a daughter fair,
So buxom, blithe, and debonair.
Haste thee, Nymph, and bring with thee
Jest, and youthful Jollity,
Quips, and Cranks, and wanton Wiles,
Nods and Becks, and wreathed Smiles—
Such as hang on Hebe's cheek,
And love to live in dimple sleek;
Sport, that wrinkled Care derides,
And Laughter, holding both his sides:
Come, and trip it as you go
On the light fantastic toe;
And in thy right hand lead with thee

The mountain-nymph, sweet Liberty;
And, if I give thee honour due,
Mirth, admit me of thy crew
To live with her and live with thee,
In unreproved pleasures free;
To hear the lark begin his flight,
And singing startle the dull night
From his watch-tower in the skies,
Till the dappled dawn doth rise;
Then to come, in spite of sorrow,
And at my window bid good-morrow,
Through the sweet-briar, or the vine,
Or the twisted eglantine;
While the cock, with lively din,
Scatters the rear of darkness thin,
And, to the stack or the barn-door,
Stoutly struts his dames before:
Oft listening how the hounds and horn
Cheerly rouse the slumbering Morn,
From the side of some hoar hill,
Through the high wood echoing shrill.
Sometime walking, not unseen,
By hedgerow elms, on hillocks green,
Right against the eastern gate,
Where the great Sun begins his state,
Robed in flames and amber light,
The clouds in thousand liveries dight;
While the ploughman, near at hand,
Whistles o'er the furrowed land,
And the milkmaid singeth blithe,
And the mower whets his scythe,
And every shepherd tells his tale,
Under the hawthorn in the dale.
Straight mine eye hath caught new pleasures,
Whilst the landscape round it measures;
Russet lawns, and fallows gray,
Where the nibbling flocks do stray,

71

Mountains on whose barren breast
The labouring clouds do often rest,
Meadows trim with daisies pied,
Shallow brooks, and rivers wide,
Towers and battlements it sees,
Bosomed high in tufted trees,
Where perhaps some Beauty lies,
The Cynosure of neighbouring eyes.
Hard by a cottage-chimney smokes
From betwixt two aged oaks,
Where Corydon and Thyrsis, met,
Are at their savoury dinner set
Of herbs and other country messes,
Which the neat-handed Phillis dresses;
And then in haste her bower she leaves,
With Thestylis to bind the sheaves;
Or, if the earlier season lead,
To the tanned haycock in the mead.
    Sometimes, with secure delight,
The upland hamlets will invite,
When the merry bells ring round,
And the jocund rebecks sound,
To many a youth and many a maid,
Dancing in the chequered shade,
And young and old come forth to play
On a sunshine holiday,
Till the live-long daylight fail;
Then to the spicy nut-brown ale,
With stories told of many a feat,
How faery Mab the junkets eat;
She was pinched and pulled, she said;
And he, by Friar's lantern led,
Tells how the drudging goblin sweat,
To earn his cream-bowl duly set,
When in one night, ere glimpse of morn,
His shadowy flail hath threshed the corn
That ten day-labourers could not end;

Then lies him down, the lubber-fiend,
And, stretched out all the chimney's length,
Basks at the fire his hairy strength,
And crop-full out of doors he flings,
Ere the first cock his matin rings.
Thus done the tales, to bed they creep,
By whispering winds soon lulled asleep.

Towered cities please us then,
And the busy hum of men,
Where throngs of knights and barons bold,
In weeds of peace, high triumphs hold,
With store of ladies, whose bright eyes
Rain influence, and judge the prize
Of wit or arms, while both contend
To win her grace, whom all commend.
There let Hymen oft appear
In saffron robe, with taper clear,
And pomp, and feast, and revelry,
With mask and antique pageantry;
Such sights as youthful poets dream,
On summer-eves by haunted stream.
Then to the well-trod stage anon,
If Jonson's learned sock be on,
Or sweetest Shakespeare, Fancy's child,
Warble his native wood-notes wild.

And ever, against eating cares,
Lap me in soft Lydian airs,
Married to immortal verse,
Such as the meeting soul may pierce,
In notes with many a winding bout
Of linked sweetness long drawn out,
With wanton heed and giddy cunning
The melting voice through mazes running
Untwisting all the chains that tie
The hidden soul of harmony;
That Orpheus' self may heave his head,
From golden slumber on a bed

Of heaped Elysian flowers, and hear
Such strains as would have won the ear
Of Pluto, to have quite set free
His half-regained Eurydicè.
  These delights if thou canst give,
Mirth, with thee I mean to live.

51. Il Penseroso

     Hence, vain deluding Joys,
The brood of Folly without father bred!
     How little you bested,
Or fill the fixed mind with all your toys!
     Dwell in some idle brain,
And fancies fond with gaudy shapes possess,
     As thick and numberless
As the gay motes that people the sunbeams,
     Or likest hovering dreams,
The fickle pensioners of Morpheus' train.
     But hail, thou Goddess sage and holy!
Hail, divinest Melancholy,
Whose saintly visage is too bright
To hit the sense of human sight,
And therefore to our weaker view
O'erlaid with black, staid Wisdom's hue;
Black, but such as in esteem
Prince Memnon's sister might beseem,
Or that starred Ethiop queen that strove
To set her beauty's praise above
The Sea-Nymphs', and their powers offended:
Yet thou art higher far descended.
Thee bright-haired Vesta long of yore
To solitary Saturn bore;
His daughter she; in Saturn's reign
Such mixture was not held a stain.
Oft in glimmering bowers and glades

74

He met her, and in secret shades
Of woody Ida's inmost grove,
While yet there was no fear of Jove.

    Come, pensive Nun, devout and pure,
Sober, steadfast, and demure,
All in a robe of darkest grain,
Flowing with majestic train,
And sable stole of Cyprus lawn
Over thy decent shoulders drawn.
Come, but keep thy wonted state,
With even step, and musing gait,
And looks commercing with the skies,
Thy rapt soul sitting in thine eyes;
There, held in holy passion still,
Forget thyself to marble, till
With a sad, leaden, downward cast
Thou fix them on the earth as fast.
And join with thee calm Peace and Quiet,
Spare Fast, that oft with gods doth diet,
And hears the Muses in a ring
Aye round about Jove's altar sing;
And add to these retired Leisure,
That in trim gardens takes his pleasure.
But, first and chiefest, with thee bring
Him that yon soars on golden wing,
Guiding the fiery-wheeled throne,
The Cherub Contemplation;
And the mute Silence hist along,
'Less Philomel will deign a song,
In her sweetest, saddest plight,
Smoothing the rugged brow of Night;
While Cynthia checks her dragon-yoke,
Gently o'er the accustomed oak.
Sweet bird, that shunnest the noise of folly,
Most musical, most melancholy!
Thee, chantress, oft the woods among
I woo to hear thy even-song;

And missing thee I walk unseen,
On the dry, smooth-shaven green,
To behold the wandering moon,
Riding near her highest noon,
Like one that has been led astray
Through the heaven's wide pathless way,
And oft, as if her head she bowed,
Stooping through a fleecy cloud.

    Oft, on a plat of rising ground,
I hear the far-off curfew sound,
Over some wide-watered shore,
Swinging slow with sullen roar;
Or, if the air will not permit,
Some still, removed place will fit,
Where glowing embers through the room
Teach light to counterfeit a gloom,
Far from all resort of mirth,
Save the cricket on the hearth,
Or the bellman's drowsy charm,
To bless the doors from nightly harm;
Or let my lamp, at midnight-hour,
Be seen in some high, lonely tower,
Where I may oft out-watch the Bear,
With thrice great Hermes, or unsphere
The spirit of Plato, to unfold
What worlds or what vast regions hold
The immortal mind, that hath forsook
Her mansion in this fleshly nook;
And of those demons that are found
In fire, air, flood, or underground,
Whose power hath a true consent
With planet, or with element.
Sometime let gorgeous Tragedy
In sceptred pall come sweeping by,
Presenting Thebes, or Pelops' line,
Or the tale of Troy divine,
Or what, though rare, of later age

Ennobled hath the buskined stage.
But, O sad Virgin! that thy power
Might raise Musaeus from his bower,
Or bid the soul of Orpheus sing
Such notes as warbled to the string
Drew iron tears down Pluto's cheek,
And made Hell grant what love did seek;
Or call up him that left half-told
The story of Cambuscan bold,
Of Camball, and of Algarsife,
And who had Canacè to wife,
That owned the virtuous ring and glass;
And of the wondrous horse of brass,
On which the Tartar king did ride;
And if ought else great bards beside
In sage and solemn tunes have sung,
Of tourneys and of trophies hung,
Of forests and enchantments drear,
Where more is meant than meets the ear.

Thus, Night, oft see me in thy pale career,
Till civil-suited Morn appear,
Not tricked and frounced, as she was wont
With the Attic boy to hunt,
But kerchiefed in a comely cloud,
While rocking winds are piping loud,
Or ushered with a shower still,
When the gust hath blown his fill,
Ending on the rustling leaves,
With minute-drops from off the eaves.

And when the sun begins to fling
His flaring beams, me, Goddess, bring
To arched walks of twilight groves,
And shadows brown, that Sylvan loves,
Of pine, or monumental oak,
Where the rude axe with heaved stroke
Was never heard the Nymphs to daunt,
Or fright them from their hallowed haunt

77

There, in close covert by some brook,
Where no profaner eye may look,
Hide me from day's garish eye,
While the bee with honeyed thigh,
That at her flowery work doth sing,
And the waters murmuring,
With such concert as they keep,
Entice the dewy-feathered Sleep.
And let some strange, mysterious dream
Wave at his wings, in aery stream
Of lively portraiture displayed,
Softly on my eyelids laid;
And, as I wake, sweet music breathe
Above, about, or underneath,
Sent by some Spirit to mortals good,
Or the unseen Genius of the wood.

    But let my due feet never fail
To walk the studious cloisters pale,
And love the high embowed roof,
With antic pillars massy-proof
And storied windows richly dight,
Casting a dim religious light.
There let the pealing organ blow,
To the full-voiced quire below,
In service high, and anthems clear,
As may with sweetness, through mine ear,
Dissolve me into ecstasies,
And bring all Heaven before mine eyes.

    And may at last my weary age
Find out the peaceful hermitage,
The hairy gown and mossy cell,
Where I may sit, and rightly spell
Of every star that heaven doth shew,
And every herb that sips the dew;
Till old experience do attain
To something like prophetic strain.

    These pleasures, Melancholy, give,
And I with thee will choose to live.

52. Lycidas

In this Monody the author bewails a learned friend,
unfortunately drowned in his passage from Chester, on the
Irish Sea, 1637; and by occasion foretells the ruin of our
corrupted clergy, then in their height.

Yet once more, O ye laurels, and once more
Ye myrtles brown, with ivy never-sere,
I come to pluck your berries harsh and crude,
And with forced fingers rude
Shatter your leaves before the mellowing year.
Bitter constraint, and sad occasion dear,
Compel me to disturb your season due;
For Lycidas is dead, dead ere his prime,
Young Lycidas, and hath not left his peer.
Who would not sing for Lycidas? he knew
Himself to sing, and build the lofty rime.
He must not float upon his watery bier
Unwept, and welter to the parching wind,
Without the meed of some melodious tear.
Begin then, Sisters of the sacred well,
That from beneath the seat of Jove doth spring;
Begin, and somewhat loudly sweep the string.
Hence with denial vain, and coy excuse—
So may some gentle Muse
With lucky words favour my destined urn,
And as he passes turn,
And bid fair peace be to my sable shroud—
For we were nursed upon the self-same hill,
Fed the same flock by fountain, shade, and rill;
Together both, ere the high lawns appeared
Under the opening eyelids of the Morn,
We drove a-field, and both together heard
What time the grey-fly winds her sultry horn,
Battening our flocks with the fresh dews of night,

Oft till the star that rose at evening, bright,
Toward heaven's descent had sloped his westering wheel.
Meanwhile the rural ditties were not mute,
Tempered to the oaten flute;
Rough Satyrs danced, and Fauns with cloven heel
From the glad sound would not be absent long,
And old Damœtas loved to hear our song.

But oh! the heavy change, now thou art gone,
Now thou art gone, and never must return!
Thee, Shepherd, thee the woods and desert caves,
With wild thyme and the gadding vine o'ergrown,
And all their echoes mourn.
The willows, and the hazel-copses green,
Shall now no more be seen
Fanning their joyous leaves to thy soft lays.
As killing as the canker to the rose,
Or taint-worm to the weanling herds that graze,
Or frost to flowers, that their gay wardrobe wear,
When first the white-thorn blows;
Such, Lycidas, thy loss to shepherds' ear.

Where were ye, Nymphs, when the remorseless deep
Closed o'er the head of your loved Lycidas?
For neither were ye playing on the steep,
Where your old bards, the famous Druids, lie,
Nor on the shaggy top of Mona high,
Nor yet where Deva spreads her wizard stream.
Ay me, I fondly dream!
Had ye been there ... for what could that have done?
What could the Muse herself that Orpheus bore,
The Muse herself for her enchanting son,
Whom universal Nature did lament,
When, by the rout that made the hideous roar,
His gory visage down the stream was sent,
Down the swift Hebrus to the Lesbian shore?

Alas! what boots it with incessant care
To tend the homely, slighted shepherd's trade,
And strictly meditate the thankless Muse?

Were it not better done, as others use,
To sport with Amaryllis in the shade,
Or with the tangles of Neaera's hair?
Fame is the spur that the clear spirit doth raise
—That last infirmity of noble mind—
To scorn delights, and live laborious days;
But the fair guerdon when we hope to find,
And think to burst out into sudden blaze,
Comes the blind Fury with the abhorred shears,
And slits the thin-spun life. 'But not the praise,'
Phœbus replied, and touched my trembling ears.
'Fame is no plant that grows on mortal soil,
Nor in the glistering foil
Set-off to the world, nor in broad rumour lies,
But lives and spreads aloft by those pure eyes,
And perfect witness of all-judging Jove;
As he pronounces lastly on each deed,
Of so much fame in Heaven expect thy meed.'

 O fountain Arethuse, and thou honoured flood,
Smooth-sliding Mincius, crowned with vocal reeds,
That strain I heard was of a higher mood.
But now my oat proceeds,
And listens to the herald of the sea,
That came in Neptune's plea.
He asked the waves, and asked the felon winds,
What hard mishap hath doomed this gentle swain?
And questioned every gust of rugged wings,
That blows from off each beaked promontory.
They knew not of his story;
And sage Hippotades their answer brings,
That not a blast was from his dungeon strayed;
The air was calm, and on the level brine
Sleek Panopè with all her sisters played.
It was that fatal and perfidious bark,
Built in the eclipse, and rigged with curses dark,
That sunk so low that sacred head of thine.

 Next Camus, reverend sire, went footing slow,

His mantle hairy and his bonnet sedge,
Inwrought with figures dim, and on the edge
Like to that sanguine flower inscribed with woe.
'Ah! who hath reft,' quoth he, 'my dearest pledge?'
Last came, and last did go,
The pilot of the Galilean lake;
Two massy keys he bore of metals twain —
The golden opes, the iron shuts amain.
He shook his mitred locks, and stern bespake:
'How well could I have spared for thee, young swain,
Enow of such as, for their bellies' sake,
Creep, and intrude, and climb into the fold!
Of other care they little reckoning make,
Than how to scramble at the shearers' feast,
And shove away the worthy bidden guest.
Blind mouths! that scarce themselves know how to hold
A sheep-hook, or have learned aught else the least
That to the faithful herdman's art belongs!
What recks it them? What need they? They are sped;
And, when they list, their lean and flashy songs
Grate on their scrannel pipes of wretched straw;
The hungry sheep look up, and are not fed,
But, swollen with wind and the rank mist they draw,
Rot inwardly, and foul contagion spread;
Beside what the grim wolf with privy paw
Daily devours apace, and nothing said.
But that two-handed engine at the door
Stands ready to smite once, and smite no more.'
    Return, Alpheüs, the dread voice is past,
That shrunk thy streams; return, Sicilian Muse,
And call the vales, and bid them hither cast
Their bells, and flowerets of a thousand hues.
Ye valleys low, where the mild whispers use
Of shades, and wanton winds, and gushing brooks,
On whose fresh lap the swart-star sparely looks;
Throw hither all your quaint-enamelled eyes,
That on the green turf suck the honeyed showers,

And purple all the ground with vernal flowers.
Bring the rathe primrose that forsaken dies,
The tufted crow-toe, and pale jessamine,
The white pink, and the pansy freaked with jet,
The glowing violet,
The musk-rose, and the well-attired woodbine,
With cowslips wan that hang the pensive head,
And every flower that sad embroidery wears;
Bid amaranthus all his beauty shed,
And daffadillies fill their cups with tears,
To strew the laureate herse where Lycid lies.
For so, to interpose a little ease,
Let our frail thoughts dally with false surmise,
Ay me! whilst thee the shores and sounding seas
Wash far away, where'er thy bones are hurled;
Whether beyond the stormy Hebrides,
Where thou perhaps under the whelming tide
Visitest the bottom of the monstrous world;
Or whether thou, to our moist vows denied,
Sleepest by the fable of Bellerus old,
Where the great Vision of the guarded mount
Looks towards Namancos and Bayona's hold....
Look homeward, Angel, now, and melt with ruth;
And, O ye dolphins, waft the hapless youth.

    Weep no more, woful shepherds, weep no more,
For Lycidas, your sorrow, is not dead,
Sunk though he be beneath the watery floor.
So sinks the day-star in the ocean-bed,
And yet anon repairs his drooping head,
And tricks his beams, and with new-spangled ore
Flames in the forehead of the morning sky:
So Lycidas sunk low, but mounted high,
Through the dear might of Him that walked the waves,
Where, other groves and other streams along,
With nectar pure his oozy locks he laves,
And hears the unexpressive nuptial song,
In the blest kingdoms meek of joy and love.

There entertain him all the saints above,
In solemn troops, and sweet societies,
That sing, and singing in their glory move,
And wipe the tears for ever from his eyes.
Now, Lycidas, the shepherds weep no more;
Henceforth thou art the Genius of the shore,
In thy large recompense, and shalt be good
To all that wander in that perilous flood.

    Thus sang the uncouth swain to the oaks and rills,
While the still Morn went out with sandals gray;
He touched the tender stops of various quills,
With eager thought warbling his Doric lay;
And now the sun had stretched out all the hills,
And now was dropped into the western bay.
At last he rose, and twitched his mantle blue;
To-morrow to fresh woods, and pastures new.

53. On His Blindness

When I consider how my light is spent
    Ere half my days, in this dark world and wide,
    And that one talent, which is death to hide,
    Lodged with me useless, though my soul more bent
To serve therewith my Maker, and present
    My true account, lest He, returning, chide;
    'Doth God exact day-labour, light denied?'
    I fondly ask. But Patience, to prevent
That murmur, soon replies: 'God doth not need
    Either man's work or his own gifts. Who best
    Bear his mild yoke, they serve him best. His state
Is kingly. Thousands, at his bidding, speed
    And post o'er land and ocean, without rest;
    They also serve who only stand and wait.'

Keightley's Text

LADY NAIRNE

54. The Land o' the Leal

I'm wearin' awa', John,
Like snaw when it's thaw, John,
I'm wearin' awa'
    To the land o' the leal.

There's nae sorrow there, John,
There's neither cauld nor care, John,
The day's aye fair
    In the land o' the leal.

Our bonnie bairn's there, John,
She was baith gude and fair, John,
And oh! we grudged her sair
    To the land o' the leal.

But sorrow's sel' wears past, John,
And joy is comin' fast, John,
The joy that's aye to last
    In the land o' the leal.

Sae dear's that joy was bought, John,
Sae free the battle fought, John,
That sinfu' man e'er brought
    To the land o' the leal.

Oh! dry your glist'ning e'e, John,
My soul langs to be free, John,
And angels beckon me
    To the land o' the leal.

Noo, haud ye leal and true, John,
Your day it's weel near through, John,

And I'll welcome you
  To the land o' the leal.

Noo, fare-ye-weel, my ain John,
This warld's cares are vain, John,
We'll meet, and we'll be fain,
  In the land o' the leal.

  Henderson's Text

ALEXANDER POPE

55. Ode on Solitude

Happy the man, whose wish and care
  A few paternal acres bound,
Content to breathe his native air,
    In his own ground.

Whose herds with milk, whose fields with bread,
  Whose flocks supply him with attire,
Whose trees in summer yield him shade,
    In winter fire.

Blest, who can unconcern'dly find
  Hours, days, and years slide soft away,
In health of body, peace of mind,
    Quiet by day.

Sound sleep by night; study and ease,
  Together mix'd; sweet recreation;
And innocence, which most does please
    With meditation.

Thus let me live, unseen, unknown,

Thus unlamented let me die,
Steal from the world, and not a stone
Tell where I lie.

1735 Edition

SIR WALTER RALEIGH

56. The Night before his Death

Even such is time, that takes on trust
Our youth, our joys, our all we have,
And pays us but with age and dust;
Who in the dark and silent grave,
When we have wandered all our ways,
Shuts up the story of our days!
But from this earth, this grave, this dust,
The Lord shall raise me up, I trust!

1829 Edition

SAMUEL ROGERS

57. A Wish

Mine be a cot beside the hill;
A bee-hive's hum shall soothe my ear;
A willowy brook, that turns a mill,
With many a fall shall linger near.

The swallow, oft, beneath my thatch,
Shall twitter from her clay-built nest;
Oft shall the pilgrim lift the latch,
And share my meal, a welcome guest.

Around my ivied porch shall spring
Each fragrant flower that drinks the dew;
And Lucy, at her wheel, shall sing
In russet-gown and apron blue.

The village-church, among the trees,
Where first our marriage-vows were given,
With merry peals shall swell the breeze,
And point with taper spire to heaven.

1846 Edition

WILLIAM SHAKESPEARE

58. Sonnets

XVII

Who will believe my verse in time to come,
If it were fill'd with your most high deserts?
Though yet, heaven knows, it is but as a tomb
Which hides your life and shows not half your parts.
If I could write the beauty of your eyes
And in fresh numbers number all your graces,
The age to come would say 'This poet lies;
Such heavenly touches ne'er touch'd earthly faces.'
So should my papers, yellowed with their age,
Be scorn'd, like old men of less truth than tongue,
And your true rights be term'd a poet's rage
And stretched metre of an antique song:
But were some child of yours alive that time,
You should live twice, in it and in my rhyme.

88

59. Shall I compare thee to a summer's day?

XVIII

Shall I compare thee to a summer's day?
Thou art more lovely and more temperate:
Rough winds do shake the darling buds of May,
And summer's lease hath all too short a date:
Sometime too hot the eye of heaven shines,
And often is his gold complexion dimm'd;
And every fair from fair sometime declines,
By chance or nature's changing course untrimm'd;
But thy eternal summer shall not fade,
Nor lose possession of that fair thou owest;
Nor shall Death brag thou wander'st in his shade,
When in eternal lines to time thou grow'st:
    So long as men can breathe, or eyes can see,
    So long lives this, and this gives life to thee.

60. When to the sessions

XXX

When to the sessions of sweet silent thought
I summon up remembrance of things past,
I sigh the lack of many a thing I sought,
And with old woes new wail my dear time's waste:
Then can I drown an eye, unused to flow,
For precious friends hid in death's dateless night,
And weep afresh love's long since cancell'd woe,
And moan the expense of many a vanish'd sight:
Then can I grieve at grievances foregone,
And heavily from woe to woe tell o'er
The sad account of fore-bemoaned moan,
Which I new pay as if not paid before.
    But if the while I think on thee, dear friend,
    All losses are restored and sorrows end.

61. Full many a glorious morning

XXXIII

Full many a glorious morning have I seen
Flatter the mountain-tops with sovereign eye,
Kissing with golden face the meadows green,
Gilding pale streams with heavenly alchemy;
Anon permit the basest clouds to ride
With ugly rack on his celestial face,
And from the forlorn world his visage hide,
Stealing unseen to west with this disgrace:
Even so my sun one early morn did shine
With all-triumphant splendour on my brow;
But, out, alack! he was but one hour mine,
The region cloud hath mask'd him from me now.
　　Yet him for this my love no whit disdaineth;
　　Suns of the world may stain when heaven's sun staineth.

62. Like as the waves

LX

Like as the waves make towards the pebbled shore,
So do our minutes hasten to their end;
Each changing place with that which goes before,
In sequent toil all forwards do contend.
Nativity, once in the main of light,
Crawls to maturity, wherewith being crown'd,
Crooked eclipses 'gainst his glory fight,
And Time that gave doth now his gift confound.
Time doth transfix the flourish set on youth
And delves the parallels in beauty's brow,
Feeds on the rarities of nature's truth,
And nothing stands but for his scythe to mow:
　　And yet to times in hope my verse shall stand,
　　Praising thy worth, despite his cruel hand.

63. Tired with all these

LXVI

Tired with all these, for restful death I cry,
As, to behold desert a beggar born,
And needy nothing trimm'd in jollity,
And purest faith unhappily forsworn,
And gilded honour shamefully misplaced,
And maiden virtue rudely strumpeted,
And right perfection wrongfully disgraced,
And strength by limping sway disabled,
And art made tongue-tied by authority,
And folly, doctor-like, controlling skill,
And simple truth miscall'd simplicity,
And captive good attending captain ill:
    Tired with all these, from these would I be gone,
    Save that, to die, I leave my love alone.

64. No longer mourn

LXXI

No longer mourn for me when I am dead
Than you shall hear the surly sullen bell
Give warning to the world that I am fled
From this vile world, with vilest worms to dwell:
Nay, if you read this line, remember not
The hand that writ it; for I love you so,
That I in your sweet thoughts would be forgot,
If thinking on me then should make you woe.
O, if, I say, you look upon this verse
When I perhaps compounded am with clay,
Do not so much as my poor name rehearse,
But let your love even with my life decay;
    Lest the wise world should look into your moan,
    And mock you with me after I am gone.

65. That time of year

LXXIII

That time of year thou mayst in me behold
When yellow leaves, or none, or few, do hang
Upon those boughs which shake against the cold,
Bare ruin'd choirs, where late the sweet birds sang.
In me thou see'st the twilight of such day
As after sunset fadeth in the west;
Which by and by black night doth take away,
Death's second self, that seals up all in rest.
In me thou see'st the glowing of such fire,
That on the ashes of his youth doth lie,
As the death-bed whereon it must expire,
Consumed with that which it was nourish'd by.
    This thou perceivest, which makes thy love more strong,
    To love that well which thou must leave ere long.

66. But be contented

LXXIV

But be contented: when that fell arrest
Without all bail shall carry me away,
My life hath in this line some interest,
Which for memorial still with thee shall stay.
When thou reviewest this, thou dost review
The very part was consecrate to thee:
The earth can have but earth, which is his due;
My spirit is thine, the better part of me:
So then thou hast but lost the dregs of life,
The prey of worms, my body being dead;
The coward conquest of a wretch's knife,
Too base of thee to be remembered.
    The worth of that is that which it contains,
    And that is this, and this with thee remains.

67. When in the chronicle

CVI

When in the chronicle of wasted time
I see descriptions of the fairest wights,
And beauty making beautiful old rhyme
In praise of ladies dead and lovely knights,
Then, in the blazon of sweet beauty's best,
Of hand, of foot, of lip, of eye, of brow,
I see their antique pen would have express'd
Even such a beauty as you master now.
So all their praises are but prophecies
Of this our time, all you prefiguring;
And, for they look'd but with divining eyes,
They had not skill enough your worth to sing:
    For we, which now behold these present days,
    Have eyes to wonder, but lack tongues to praise.

68. Let me not to the marriage

CXVI

Let me not to the marriage of true minds
Admit impediments. Love is not love
Which alters when it alteration finds,
Or bends with the remover to remove:
O, no! it is an ever-fixed mark,
That looks on tempests and is never shaken;
It is the star to every wandering bark,
Whose worth's unknown, although his height be taken.
Love's not Time's fool, though rosy lips and cheeks
Within his bending sickle's compass come;
Love alters not with his brief hours and weeks,
But bears it out even to the edge of doom.
    If this be error and upon me proved,
    I never writ, nor no man ever loved.

69. Song from 'The Tempest.'

Full fathom five thy father lies;
Of his bones are coral made;
Those are pearls that were his eyes:
Nothing of him that doth fade,
But doth suffer a sea-change
Into something rich and strange.
Sea-nymphs hourly ring his knell:
Ding-dong.
Hark! now I hear them,—
Ding-dong, bell.

70. Song from 'Measure for Measure.'

Take, O, take those lips away,
That so sweetly were forsworn;
And those eyes, the break of day,
Lights that do mislead the morn:
But my kisses bring again, bring again;
Seals of love, but seal'd in vain, seal'd in vain.

71. Song from 'Much Ado about Nothing.'

Sigh no more, ladies, sigh no more,
Men were deceivers ever,
One foot in sea and one on shore,
To one thing constant never:
Then sigh not so, but let them go,
And be you blithe and bonny,
Converting all your sounds of woe
Into Hey nonny, nonny.

Sing no more ditties, sing no moe,
Of dumps so dull and heavy;
The fraud of men was ever so,

Since summer first was leavy:
Then sigh not so, but let them go,
    And be you blithe and bonny,
Converting all your sounds of woe
    Into Hey nonny, nonny.

72. Song from 'Cymbeline.'

Fear no more the heat o' the sun,
    Nor the furious winter's rages;
Thou thy worldly task hast done,
    Home art gone and ta'en thy wages:
Golden lads and girls all must,
As chimney-sweepers, come to dust.

Fear no more the frown o' the great;
    Thou art past the tyrant's stroke;
Care no more to clothe and eat;
    To thee the reed is as the oak:
The sceptre, learning, physic, must
All follow this and come to dust.

Fear no more the lightning-flash,
    Nor the all-dreaded thunder-stone;
Fear not slander, censure rash;
    Thou hast finish'd joy and moan:
All lovers young, all lovers must
Consign to thee and come to dust.

No exorciser harm thee!
Nor no witchcraft charm thee!
Ghost unlaid forbear thee!
Nothing ill come near thee!
Quiet consummation have;
And renowned be thy grave!

                    Cambridge Shakespeare Text

PERCY BYSSHE SHELLEY

73. Song from 'Prometheus Unbound'

On a poet's lips I slept
Dreaming like a love-adept
In the sound his breathing kept;
Nor seeks nor finds he mortal blisses
But feeds on the aërial kisses
Of shapes that haunt thought's wildernesses.
He will watch from dawn to gloom
The lake-reflected sun illume
The yellow bees in the ivy-bloom,
Nor heed nor see, what things they be;
But from these create he can
Forms more real than living man,
Nurslings of immortality!
One of these awakened me,
And I sped to succour thee.

74. Ode to the West Wind

I

O wild West Wind, thou breath of Autumn's being,
Thou, from whose unseen presence the leaves dead
Are driven, like ghosts from an enchanter fleeing,

Yellow, and black, and pale, and hectic red,
Pestilence-stricken multitudes: O, thou,
Who chariotest to their dark wintry bed

The wingèd seeds, where they lie cold and low,
Each like a corpse within its grave, until
Thine azure sister of the spring shall blow

Her clarion o'er the dreaming earth, and fill
(Driving sweet buds like flocks to feed in air)
With living hues and odours plain and hill:

Wild Spirit, which art moving every where;
Destroyer and preserver; hear, O, hear!

II

Thou on whose stream, 'mid the steep sky's commotion,
Loose clouds like earth's decaying leaves are shed,
Shook from the tangled boughs of Heaven and Ocean,

Angels of rain and lightning: there are spread
On the blue surface of thine airy surge,
Like the bright hair uplifted from the head

Of some fierce Maenad, even from the dim verge
Of the horizon to the zenith's height
The locks of the approaching storm. Thou dirge

Of the dying year, to which this closing night
Will be the dome of a vast sepulchre,
Vaulted with all thy congregated might

Of vapours, from whose solid atmosphere
Black rain, and fire, and hail will burst: O, hear!

III

Thou who didst waken from his summer dreams
The blue Mediterranean, where he lay,
Lulled by the coil of his crystalline streams,

Beside a pumice isle in Baiae's bay,
And saw in sleep old palaces and towers
Quivering within the wave's intenser day,

All overgrown with azure moss and flowers
So sweet, the sense faints picturing them! Thou
For whose path the Atlantic's level powers

Cleave themselves into chasms, while far below
The sea-blooms and the oozy woods which wear
The sapless foliage of the ocean, know

Thy voice, and suddenly grow gray with fear,
And tremble and despoil themselves: O, hear!

IV

If I were a dead leaf thou mightest bear;
If I were a swift cloud to fly with thee;
A wave to pant beneath thy power, and share

The impulse of thy strength, only less free
Than thou, O, uncontroulable! If even
I were as in my boyhood, and could be

The comrade of thy wanderings over heaven,
As then, when to outstrip thy skiey speed
Scarce seemed a vision; I would ne'er have striven

As thus with thee in prayer in my sore need.
O! lift me as a wave, a leaf, a cloud!
I fall upon the thorns of life! I bleed!

A heavy weight of hours has chained and bowed
One too like thee: tameless, and swift, and proud.

V

Make me thy lyre, even as the forest is:
What if my leaves are falling like its own!
The tumult of thy mighty harmonies

Will take from both a deep, autumnal tone,
Sweet though in sadness. Be thou, spirit fierce,
My spirit! Be thou me, impetuous one!

Drive my dead thoughts over the universe
Like withered leaves to quicken a new birth!
And, by the incantation of this verse,

Scatter, as from an unextinguished hearth
Ashes and sparks, my words among mankind!
Be through my lips to unawakened earth

The trumpet of a prophecy! O, wind,
If Winter comes, can Spring be far behind?

75. The Cloud

I bring fresh showers for the thirsting flowers,
    From the seas and the streams;
I bear light shade for the leaves when laid
    In their noon-day dreams.
From my wings are shaken the dews that waken
    The sweet buds every one,
When rocked to rest on their mother's breast,
    As she dances about the sun.
I wield the flail of the lashing hail,
    And whiten the green plains under,
And then again I dissolve it in rain,
    And laugh as I pass in thunder.

I sift the snow on the mountains below,
    And their great pines groan aghast;
And all the night 'tis my pillow white,
    While I sleep in the arms of the blast.
Sublime on the towers of my skiey bowers,
    Lightning my pilot sits,

In a cavern under is fettered the thunder,
 It struggles and howls at fits;
Over earth and ocean, with gentle motion,
 This pilot is guiding me,
Lured by the love of the genii that move
 In the depths of the purple sea;
Over the rills, and the crags, and the hills,
 Over the lakes and the plains,
Wherever he dream, under mountain or stream,
 The Spirit he loves remains;
And I all the while bask in heaven's blue smile,
 Whilst he is dissolving in rains.

The sanguine sunrise, with his meteor eyes,
 And his burning plumes outspread,
Leaps on the back of my sailing rack,
 When the morning star shines dead,
As on the jag of a mountain crag,
 Which an earthquake rocks and swings,
An eagle alit one moment may sit
 In the light of its golden wings.
And when sunset may breathe, from the lit sea beneath,
 Its ardours of rest and of love,
And the crimson pall of eve may fall
 From the depth of heaven above,
With wings folded I rest, on mine airy nest,
 As still as a brooding dove.

That orbèd maiden with white fire laden,
 Whom mortals call the moon,
Glides glimmering o'er my fleece-like floor,
 By the midnight breezes strewn;
And wherever the beat of her unseen feet,
 Which only the angels hear,
May have broken the woof of my tent's thin roof,
 The stars peep behind her and peer;
And I laugh to see them whirl and flee,

100

Like a swarm of golden bees,
When I widen the rent in my wind-built tent,
Till the calm rivers, lakes, and seas,
Like strips of the sky fallen through me on high,
Are each paved with the moon and these.

I bind the sun's throne with a burning zone,
And the moon's with a girdle of pearl;
The volcanoes are dim, and the stars reel and swim,
When the whirlwinds my banner unfurl.
From cape to cape, with a bridge-like shape,
Over a torrent sea,
Sunbeam-proof, I hang like a roof,
The mountains its columns be.
The triumphal arch through which I march
With hurricane, fire, and snow,
When the powers of the air are chained to my chair,
Is the million-coloured bow;
The sphere-fire above its soft colours wove,
While the moist earth was laughing below.

I am the daughter of earth and water,
And the nursling of the sky;
I pass through the pores of the ocean and shores;
I change, but I cannot die.
For after the rain when with never a stain,
The pavilion of heaven is bare,
And the winds and sunbeams with their convex gleams,
Build up the blue dome of air,
I silently laugh at my own cenotaph,
And out of the caverns of rain,
Like a child from the womb, like a ghost from the tomb,
I arise and unbuild it again.

76. To a Skylark

Hail to thee, blithe spirit!
Bird thou never wert,
That from heaven, or near it,
Pourest thy full heart
In profuse strains of unpremeditated art.

Higher still and higher
From the earth thou springest
Like a cloud of fire;
The blue deep thou wingest,
And singing still dost soar, and soaring ever singest.

In the golden lightning
Of the sunken sun,
O'er which clouds are brightning,
Thou dost float and run;
Like an unbodied joy whose race is just begun.

The pale purple even
Melts around thy flight;
Like a star of heaven,
In the broad day-light
Thou art unseen, but yet I hear thy shrill delight,

Keen as are the arrows
Of that silver sphere,
Whose intense lamp narrows
In the white dawn clear,
Until we hardly see, we feel that it is there.

All the earth and air
With thy voice is loud,
As, when night is bare,
From one lonely cloud
The moon rains out her beams, and heaven is overflowed.

What thou art we know not;
What is most like thee?
From rainbow clouds there flow not
Drops so bright to see,
As from thy presence showers a rain of melody.

Like a poet hidden
In the light of thought,
Singing hymns unbidden,
Till the world is wrought
To sympathy with hopes and fears it heeded not:

Like a high-born maiden
In a palace tower,
Soothing her love-laden
Soul in secret hour
With music sweet as love, which overflows her bower:

Like a glow-worm golden
In a dell of dew,
Scattering unbeholden
Its aërial hue
Among the flowers and grass, which screen it from the view:

Like a rose embowered
In its own green leaves,
By warm winds deflowered,
Till the scent it gives
Makes faint with too much sweet these heavy-winged thieves:

Sound of vernal showers
On the twinkling grass,
Rain-awakened flowers,
All that ever was
Joyous, and clear, and fresh, thy music doth surpass:

Teach us, sprite or bird,

What sweet thoughts are thine:
I have never heard
Praise of love or wine
That panted forth a flood of rapture so divine.

Chorus Hymenaeal,
Or triumphal chaunt,
Matched with thine would be all
But an empty vaunt,
A thing wherein we feel there is some hidden want.

What objects are the fountains
Of thy happy strain?
What fields, or waves, or mountains?
What shapes of sky or plain?
What love of thine own kind? what ignorance of pain?

With thy clear keen joyance
Languor cannot be:
Shadow of annoyance
Never came near thee:
Thou lovest; but ne'er knew love's sad satiety.

Waking or asleep,
Thou of death must deem
Things more true and deep
Than we mortals dream,
Or how could thy notes flow in such a crystal stream?

We look before and after,
And pine for what is not:
Our sincerest laughter
With some pain is fraught;
Our sweetest songs are those that tell of saddest thought.

Yet if we could scorn
Hate, and pride, and fear;

104

If we were things born
Not to shed a tear,
I know not how thy joy we ever should come near.

Better than all measures
Of delightful sound,
Better than all treasures
That in books are found,
Thy skill to poet were, thou scorner of the ground!

Teach me half the gladness
That thy brain must know,
Such harmonious madness
From my lips would flow,
The world should listen then, as I am listening now.

77. Chorus from 'Hellas.'

The world's great age begins anew,
The golden years return,
The earth doth like a snake renew
Her winter weeds outworn:
Heaven smiles, and faiths and empires gleam,
Like wrecks of a dissolving dream.

A brighter Hellas rears its mountains
From waves serener far;
A new Peneus rolls his fountains
Against the morning-star.
Where fairer Tempes bloom, there sleep
Young Cyclads on a sunnier deep.

A loftier Argo cleaves the main,
Fraught with a later prize;
Another Orpheus sings again,
And loves, and weeps, and dies.

A new Ulysses leaves once more
Calypso for his native shore.

O, write no more the tale of Troy,
  If earth Death's scroll must be!
Nor mix with Laian rage the joy
  Which dawns upon the free:
Although a subtler Sphinx renew
Riddles of death Thebes never knew.

Another Athens shall arise,
  And to remoter time
Bequeath, like sunset to the skies,
  The splendour of its prime;
And leave, if nought so bright may live,
All earth can take or Heaven can give.

Saturn and Love their long repose
  Shall burst, more bright and good
Than all who fell, than One who rose,
  Than many unsubdued:
Not gold, not blood, their altar dowers,
But votive tears and symbol flowers.

O cease! must hate and death return?
  Cease! must men kill and die?
Cease! drain not to its dregs the urn
  Of bitter prophecy.
The world is weary of the past,
O might it die or rest at last!

106

78. Stanzas. Written in Dejection, near Naples

I

The sun is warm, the sky is clear,
  The waves are dancing fast and bright,
Blue isles and snowy mountains wear
  The purple noon's transparent might,
  The breath of the moist earth is light,
Around its unexpanded buds;
  Like many a voice of one delight,
The winds, the birds, the ocean floods,
The City's voice itself is soft like Solitude's.

II

I see the Deep's untrampled floor
  With green and purple seaweeds strown;
I see the waves upon the shore,
  Like light dissolved in star-showers, thrown:
  I sit upon the sands alone,
The lightning of the noon-tide ocean
  Is flashing round me, and a tone
Arises from its measured motion,
How sweet! did any heart now share in my emotion.

III

Alas! I have nor hope nor health,
  Nor peace within nor calm around,
Nor that content surpassing wealth
  The sage in meditation found,
  And walked with inward glory crowned—
Nor fame, nor power, nor love, nor leisure.
  Others I see whom these surround—
  Smiling they live and call life pleasure;—
To me that cup has been dealt in another measure.

IV

Yet now despair itself is mild,

Even as the winds and waters are;
I could lie down like a tired child,
And weep away the life of care
Which I have borne and yet must bear,
Till death like sleep might steal on me,
And I might feel in the warm air
My cheek grow cold, and hear the sea
Breathe o'er my dying brain its last monotony.

V

Some might lament that I were cold,
As I, when this sweet day is gone,
Which my lost heart, too soon grown old,
Insults with this untimely moan;
They might lament—for I am one
Whom men love not,—and yet regret,
Unlike this day, which, when the sun
Shall in its stainless glory set,
Will linger, though enjoyed, like joy in memory yet.

79. The Indian Serenade

I

I arise from dreams of thee
In the first sweet sleep of night,
When the winds are breathing low,
And the stars are shining bright:
I arise from dreams of thee,
And a spirit in my feet
Hath led me—who knows how?
To thy chamber window, Sweet!

II

The wandering airs they faint
On the dark, the silent stream—

108

And the Champak's odours fail
Like sweet thoughts in a dream;
The nightingale's complaint,
It dies upon her heart;—
As I must on thine,
O! belovèd as thou art!

III

O lift me from the grass!
I die! I faint! I fail!
Let thy love in kisses rain
On my lips and eyelids pale.
My cheek is cold and white, alas!
My heart beats loud and fast;—
Oh! press it to thine own again,
Where it will break at last.

80. To ——

I

I fear thy kisses, gentle maiden,
 Thou needest not fear mine;
My spirit is too deeply laden
 Ever to burthen thine.

II

I fear thy mien, thy tones, thy motion,
 Thou needest not fear mine;
Innocent is the heart's devotion
 With which I worship thine.

81. To Night

I

Swiftly walk over the western wave,
Spirit of Night!
Out of the misty eastern cave,
Where all the long and lone daylight,
Thou wovest dreams of joy and fear,
Which make thee terrible and dear,—
Swift be thy flight!

II

Wrap thy form in a mantle gray,
Star-inwrought!
Blind with thine hair the eyes of Day;
Kiss her until she be wearied out,
Then wander o'er city, and sea, and land,
Touching all with thine opiate wand—
Come, long sought!

III

When I arose and saw the dawn,
I sigh'd for thee;
When light rode high, and the dew was gone,
And noon lay heavy on flower and tree,
And the weary Day turned to his rest,
Lingering like an unloved guest,
I sighed for thee.

IV

Thy brother Death came, and cried,
Wouldst thou me?
Thy sweet child Sleep, the filmy-eyed,
Murmured like a noon-tide bee,
Shall I nestle near thy side?
Wouldst thou me?—And I replied,
No, not thee!

V

Death will come when thou art dead,
*   Soon, too soon—*
Sleep will come when thou art fled;
Of neither would I ask the boon
I ask of thee, belovèd Night—
Swift be thine approaching flight,
*   Come soon, soon!*

        Buxton Forman's Text

JAMES SHIRLEY

82. Song from 'Ajax and Ulysses'

The glories of our blood and state
*   Are shadows, not substantial things;*
There is no armour against fate;
*   Death lays his icy hand on kings:*
*   Sceptre and crown*
*   Must tumble down,*
And in the dust be equal made
With the poor crooked scythe and spade.

Some men with swords may reap the field,
*   And plant fresh laurels where they kill;*
But their strong nerves at last must yield;
*   They tame but one another still:*
*   Early or late,*
*   They stoop to fate,*
And must give up their murmuring breath,
When they, pale captives, creep to death.

The garlands wither on your brow,
*   Then boast no more your mighty deeds;*
Upon Death's purple altar now,

> See, where the victor-victim bleeds:
>   Your heads must come
>   To the cold tomb,
> Only the actions of the just
> Smell sweet, and blossom in their dust.
>
> *Dyce's Text*

ROBERT SOUTHEY

83. Stanzas

1

My days among the Dead are past;
   Around me I behold,
Where'er these casual eyes are cast
   The mighty minds of old;
My never failing friends are they,
With whom I converse day by day.

2

With them I take delight in weal,
   And seek relief in woe;
And while I understand and feel
   How much to them I owe,
My cheeks have often been bedew'd
With tears of thoughtful gratitude.

3

My thoughts are with the Dead, with them
   I live in long-past years,
Their virtues love, their faults condemn,
   Partake their hopes and fears,
And from their lessons seek and find
Instruction with an humble mind.

4

My hopes are with the Dead, anon
My place with them will be,
And I with them shall travel on
Through all Futurity;
Yet leaving here a name, I trust,
That will not perish in the dust.

1837 Edition

ROBERT LOUIS STEVENSON

84. Requiem

Under the wide and starry sky,
Dig the grave and let me lie.
Glad did I live and gladly die,
And I laid me down with a will.

This be the verse you grave for me:
Here he lies where he longed to be;
Home is the sailor, home from sea,
And the hunter home from the hill.

1887 Edition

LORD TENNYSON

85. Song from 'The Miller's Daughter'

It is the miller's daughter,
And she is grown so dear, so dear,
That I would be the jewel
That trembles in her ear:
For hid in ringlets day and night,

I'd touch her neck so warm and white.

And I would be the girdle
    About her dainty dainty waist,
And her heart would beat against me,
    In sorrow and in rest:
And I should know if it beat right,
I'd clasp it round so close and tight.

And I would be the necklace,
    And all day long to fall and rise
Upon her balmy bosom,
    With her laughter or her sighs,
And I would lie so light, so light,
I scarce should be unclasp'd at night.

86. St. Agnes' Eve

Deep on the convent-roof the snows
    Are sparkling to the moon:
My breath to heaven like vapour goes:
    May my soul follow soon!
The shadows of the convent-towers
    Slant down the snowy sward,
Still creeping with the creeping hours
    That lead me to my Lord:
Make Thou my spirit pure and clear
    As are the frosty skies,
Or this first snowdrop of the year
    That in my bosom lies.

As these white robes are soil'd and dark,
    To yonder shining ground;
As this pale taper's earthly spark,
    To yonder argent round;
So shows my soul before the Lamb,

My spirit before Thee;
So in mine earthly house I am,
  To that I hope to be.
Break up the heavens, O Lord! and far,
  Thro' all yon starlight keen,
Draw me, thy bride, a glittering star,
  In raiment white and clean.

He lifts me to the golden doors;
  The flashes come and go;
All heaven bursts her starry floors,
  And strows her lights below,
And deepens on and up! the gates
  Roll back, and far within
For me the Heavenly Bridegroom waits,
  To make me pure of sin.
The sabbaths of Eternity,
  One sabbath deep and wide—
A light upon the shining sea—
  The Bridegroom with his bride!

87. Break, break, break

Break, break, break,
  On thy cold gray stones, O Sea!
And I would that my tongue could utter
  The thoughts that arise in me.

O well for the fisherman's boy,
  That he shouts with his sister at play!
O well for the sailor lad,
  That he sings in his boat on the bay!

And the stately ships go on
  To their haven under the hill;
But O for the touch of a vanish'd hand,

115

And the sound of a voice that is still!

Break, break, break,
    At the foot of thy crags, O Sea!
But the tender grace of a day that is dead
    Will never come back to me.

88. Song from 'The Princess'

    Tears, idle tears, I know not what they mean,
Tears from the depth of some divine despair
Rise in the heart, and gather to the eyes,
In looking on the happy Autumn-fields,
And thinking of the days that are no more.

    Fresh as the first beam glittering on a sail,
That brings our friends up from the underworld,
Sad as the last which reddens over one
That sinks with all we love below the verge;
So sad, so fresh, the days that are no more.

    Ah, sad and strange as in dark summer dawns
The earliest pipe of half-awaken'd birds
To dying ears, when unto dying eyes
The casement slowly grows a glimmering square;
So sad, so strange, the days that are no more.

    Dear as remember'd kisses after death,
And sweet as those by hopeless fancy feign'd
On lips that are for others; deep as love,
Deep as first love, and wild with all regret;
O Death in Life, the days that are no more.

89. Song from 'The Princess'

Ask me no more: the moon may draw the sea;
  The cloud may stoop from heaven and take the shape
  With fold to fold, of mountain or of cape;
But O too fond, when have I answer'd thee?
              Ask me no more.

Ask me no more: what answer should I give?
  I love not hollow cheek or faded eye:
  Yet, O my friend, I will not have thee die!
Ask me no more, lest I should bid thee live;
              Ask me no more.

Ask me no more: thy fate and mine are seal'd:
  I strove against the stream and all in vain:
  Let the great river take me to the main:
No more, dear love, for at a touch I yield;
              Ask me no more.

90. Crossing the Bar

Sunset and evening star,
  And one clear call for me!
And may there be no moaning of the bar,
  When I put out to sea,

But such a tide as moving seems asleep,
  Too full for sound and foam,
When that which drew from out the boundless deep
  Turns again home.

Twilight and evening bell,
  And after that the dark!
And may there be no sadness of farewell,
  When I embark;

For tho' from out our bourne of Time and Place
   The flood may bear me far,
I hope to see my Pilot face to face
   When I have crost the bar.

                   1902 Edition

EDMUND WALLER

91. On a Girdle

That which her slender waist confined,
Shall now my joyful temples bind:
No monarch but would give his crown,
His arms might do what this has done.

It was my heaven's extremest sphere,
The pale which held that lovely deer.
My joy, my grief, my hope, my love,
Did all within this circle move!

A narrow compass! and yet there
Dwelt all that's good, and all that's fair:
Give me but what this ribbon bound,
Take all the rest the sun goes round.

92. Song

   Go, lovely Rose!
Tell her that wastes her time and me,
   That now she knows,
When I resemble her to thee,
How sweet and fair she seems to be.

   Tell her that's young,
And shuns to have her graces spied,

That hadst thou sprung
In deserts, where no men abide,
Thou must have uncommended died.

Small is the worth
Of beauty from the light retired:
Bid her come forth,
Suffer herself to be desired,
And not blush so to be admired.

Then die! that she
The common fate of all things rare
May read in thee,
How small a part of time they share
That are so wondrous sweet and fair!

1822 Edition

WILLIAM WORDSWORTH

93. She dwelt among the untrodden ways

She dwelt among the untrodden ways
Beside the springs of Dove,
A Maid whom there were none to praise
And very few to love:

A violet by a mossy stone
Half hidden from the eye!
—Fair as a star, when only one
Is shining in the sky.

She lived unknown, and few could know
When Lucy ceased to be;
But she is in her grave, and, oh,
The difference to me!

119

94. She was a Phantom of delight

She was a Phantom of delight
When first she gleamed upon my sight;
A lovely Apparition, sent
To be a moment's ornament;
Her eyes as stars of Twilight fair;
Like Twilight's, too, her dusky hair;
But all things else about her drawn
From May-time and the cheerful Dawn;
A dancing Shape, an Image gay,
To haunt, to startle, and way-lay.

I saw her upon nearer view,
A Spirit, yet a Woman too!
Her household motions light and free,
And steps of virgin-liberty;
A countenance in which did meet
Sweet records, promises as sweet;
A Creature not too bright or good
For human nature's daily food;
For transient sorrows, simple wiles,
Praise, blame, love, kisses, tears, and smiles.

And now I see with eye serene
The very pulse of the machine;
A Being breathing thoughtful breath,
A Traveller between life and death;
The reason firm, the temperate will,
Endurance, foresight, strength, and skill;
A perfect Woman, nobly planned,
To warn, to comfort, and command;
And yet a Spirit still, and bright
With something of angelic light.

120

95. Sonnets

PART I—XXXIII

The world is too much with us; late and soon,
Getting and spending, we lay waste our powers:
Little we see in Nature that is ours;
We have given our hearts away, a sordid boon!
This Sea that bares her bosom to the moon;
The winds that will be howling at all hours,
And are up-gathered now like sleeping flowers;
For this, for everything, we are out of tune;
It moves us not.—Great God! I'd rather be
A Pagan suckled in a creed outworn;
So might I, standing on this pleasant lea,
Have glimpses that would make me less forlorn;
Have sight of Proteus rising from the sea;
Or hear old Triton blow his wreathèd horn.

96.

PART II—XXXVI

Composed upon Westminster Bridge, September 3, 1802.
Earth has not anything to show more fair:
Dull would be he of soul who could pass by
A sight so touching in its majesty:
This City now doth, like a garment, wear
The beauty of the morning; silent, bare,
Ships, towers, domes, theatres, and temples lie
Open unto the fields, and to the sky;
All bright and glittering in the smokeless air.
Never did sun more beautifully steep
In his first splendour, valley, rock, or hill;
Ne'er saw I, never felt, a calm so deep!
The river glideth at his own sweet will:
Dear God! the very houses seem asleep;
And all that mighty heart is lying still!

97. To a Highland Girl, at Inversneyde, upon Loch Lomond

Sweet Highland Girl, a very shower
Of beauty is thy earthly dower!
Twice seven consenting years have shed
Their utmost bounty on thy head:
And these gray rocks; that household lawn;
Those trees, a veil just half withdrawn;
This fall of water that doth make
A murmur near the silent lake;
This little bay; a quiet road
That holds in shelter thy Abode—
In truth together do ye seem
Like something fashioned in a dream;
Such Forms as from their covert peep
When earthly cares are laid asleep!
But, O fair Creature! in the light
Of common day, so heavenly bright,
I bless Thee, Vision as thou art,
I bless thee with a human heart;
God shield thee to thy latest years!
Thee, neither know I, nor thy peers;
And yet my eyes are filled with tears.

With earnest feeling I shall pray
For thee when I am far away:
For never saw I mien, or face,
In which more plainly I could trace
Benignity and home-bred sense
Ripening in perfect innocence.
Here scattered, like a random seed,
Remote from men, Thou dost not need
The embarrassed look of shy distress,
And maidenly shamefacedness:
Thou wear'st upon thy forehead clear

The freedom of a Mountaineer:
A face with gladness overspread!
Soft smiles, by human kindness bred!
And seemliness complete, that sways
Thy courtesies, about thee plays;
With no restraint, but such as springs
From quick and eager visitings
Of thoughts that lie beyond the reach
Of thy few words of English speech:
A bondage sweetly brooked, a strife
That gives thy gestures grace and life!
So have I, not unmoved in mind,
Seen birds of tempest-loving kind—
Thus beating up against the wind.

What hand but would a garland cull
For thee who art so beautiful.
O happy pleasure! here to dwell
Beside thee in some heathy dell;
Adopt your homely ways, and dress,
A Shepherd, thou a Shepherdess!
But I could frame a wish for thee
More like a grave reality:
Thou art to me but as a wave
Of the wild sea; and I would have
Some claim upon thee, if I could,
Though but of common neighbourhood.
What joy to hear thee, and to see!
Thy elder Brother I would be,
Thy Father—anything to thee!

Now thanks to Heaven! that of its grace
Hath led me to this lonely place.
Joy have I had; and going hence
I bear away my recompense.
In spots like these it is we prize
Our Memory, feel that she hath eyes:

123

Then, why should I be loth to stir?
I feel this place was made for her;
To give new pleasure like the past,
Continued long as life shall last.
Nor am I loth, though pleased at heart,
Sweet Highland Girl! from thee to part;
For I, methinks, till I grow old,
As fair before me shall behold,
As I do now, the cabin small,
The lake, the bay, the waterfall;
And Thee, the Spirit of them all!

98. The Solitary Reaper

Behold her, single in the field,
Yon solitary Highland Lass!
Reaping and singing by herself;
Stop here, or gently pass!
Alone she cuts and binds the grain,
And sings a melancholy strain;
O listen! for the Vale profound
Is overflowing with the sound.

No Nightingale did ever chaunt
More welcome notes to weary bands
Of travellers in some shady haunt,
Among Arabian sands:
A voice so thrilling ne'er was heard
In spring-time from the Cuckoo-bird,
Breaking the silence of the seas
Among the farthest Hebrides.
Will no one tell me what she sings?—
Perhaps the plaintive numbers flow
For old, unhappy, far-off things,
And battles long ago:
Or is it some more humble lay,

124

Familiar matter of to-day?
Some natural sorrow, loss, or pain,
That has been, and may be again?

Whate'er the theme, the Maiden sang
As if her song could have no ending;
I saw her singing at her work,
And o'er the sickle bending;—
I listened, motionless and still;
And, as I mounted up the hill,
The music in my heart I bore,
Long after it was heard no more.

99. Intimations of Immortality from Recollections of Early Childhood

The Child is father of the Man;
And I could wish my days to be
Bound each to each by natural piety.

I

There was a time when meadow, grove, and stream,
The earth, and every common sight,
To me did seem
Apparelled in celestial light,
The glory and the freshness of a dream.
It is not now as it hath been of yore;—
Turn wheresoe'er I may,
By night or day,
The things which I have seen I now can see no more.

II

The Rainbow comes and goes,
And lovely is the Rose,
The Moon doth with delight

125

Look round her when the heavens are bare,
  Waters on a starry night
  Are beautiful and fair;
The sunshine is a glorious birth;
But yet I know, where'er I go,
That there hath past away a glory from the earth.

III

Now, while the birds thus sing a joyous song,
  And while the young lambs bound
  As to the tabor's sound,
To me alone there came a thought of grief:
A timely utterance gave that thought relief,
  And I again am strong:
The cataracts blow their trumpets from the steep;
No more shall grief of mine the season wrong;
I hear the Echoes through the mountains throng,
The Winds come to me from the fields of sleep,
  And all the earth is gay;
    Land and sea
  Give themselves up to jollity,
  And with the heart of May
  Doth every Beast keep holiday;
    Thou Child of Joy,
Shout round me, let me hear thy shouts, thou happy Shepherd-b

IV

Ye blessèd Creatures, I have heard the call
  Ye to each other make; I see
The heavens laugh with you in your jubilee;
  My heart is at your festival,
  My head hath its coronal,
The fulness of your bliss, I feel—I feel it all.
    O evil day! if I were sullen
    While Earth herself is adorning,
      This sweet May-morning,
    And the Children are culling

On every side,
In a thousand valleys far and wide,
Fresh flowers; while the sun shines warm,
And the Babe leaps up on his Mother's arm:—
I hear, I hear, with joy I hear!
—But there's a Tree, of many, one,
A single Field which I have looked upon,
Both of them speak of something that is gone:
The Pansy at my feet
Doth the same tale repeat:
Whither is fled the visionary gleam?
Where is it now, the glory and the dream?

V

Our birth is but a sleep and a forgetting:
The Soul that rises with us, our life's Star,
Hath had elsewhere its setting,
And cometh from afar:
Not in entire forgetfulness,
And not in utter nakedness,
But trailing clouds of glory do we come
From God, who is our home:
Heaven lies about us in our infancy!
Shades of the prison-house begin to close
Upon the growing Boy,
But He beholds the light, and whence it flows,
He sees it in his joy;
The Youth, who daily farther from the east
Must travel, still is Nature's Priest,
And by the vision splendid
Is on his way attended;
At length the Man perceives it die away,
And fade into the light of common day.

VI

Earth fills her lap with pleasures of her own;
Yearnings she hath in her own natural kind,

127

And, even with something of a Mother's mind,
And no unworthy aim,
The homely Nurse doth all she can
To make her Foster-child, her Inmate Man,
Forget the glories he hath known,
And that imperial palace whence he came.

VII

Behold the Child among his new-born blisses,
A six years' Darling of a pigmy size!
See, where 'mid work of his own hand he lies,
Fretted by sallies of his mother's kisses,
With light upon him from his father's eyes!
See, at his feet, some little plan or chart,
Some fragment from his dream of human life,
Shaped by himself with newly-learned art;
A wedding or a festival,
A mourning or a funeral;
And this hath now his heart,
And unto this he frames his song:
Then will he fit his tongue
To dialogues of business, love, or strife;
But it will not be long
Ere this be thrown aside,
And with new joy and pride
The little Actor cons another part;
Filling from time to time his 'humorous stage'
With all the Persons, down to palsied Age,
That Life brings with her in her equipage;
As if his whole vocation
Were endless imitation.

VIII

Thou, whose exterior semblance doth belie
Thy Soul's immensity;
Thou best Philosopher, who yet dost keep
Thy heritage, thou Eye among the blind,

128

That, deaf and silent, read'st the eternal deep,
Haunted for ever by the eternal mind,—
            Mighty Prophet! Seer blest!
            On whom those truths do rest,
Which we are toiling all our lives to find,
In darkness lost, the darkness of the grave;
Thou, over whom thy Immortality
Broods like the Day, a Master o'er a Slave,
A Presence which is not to be put by;
            To whom the grave
Is but a lonely bed without the sense or sight
            Of day or the warm light,
A place of thought where we in waiting lie;
Thou little Child, yet glorious in the might
Of heaven-born freedom on thy being's height,
Why with such earnest pains dost thou provoke
The years to bring the inevitable yoke,
Thus blindly with thy blessedness at strife?
Full soon thy Soul shall have her earthly freight,
And custom lie upon thee with a weight
Heavy as frost, and deep almost as life!

IX

            O joy! that in our embers
            Is something that doth live,
            That nature yet remembers
What was so fugitive!
The thought of our past years in me doth breed
Perpetual benediction: not indeed
For that which is most worthy to be blest;
Delight and liberty, the simple creed
Of Childhood, whether busy or at rest,
With new-fledged hope still fluttering in his breast:—
            Not for these I raise
            The song of thanks and praise;
            But for those obstinate questionings
            Of sense and outward things,

Fallings from us, vanishings;
  Blank misgivings of a Creature
Moving about in worlds not realised,
High instincts before which our mortal Nature
Did tremble like a guilty Thing surprised:
   But for those first affections,
   Those shadowy recollections,
Which, be they what they may,
Are yet the fountain-light of all our day,
Are yet a master-light of all our seeing;
  Uphold us, cherish, and have power to make
Our noisy years seem moments in the being
Of the eternal Silence: truths that wake,
    To perish never;
Which neither listlessness, nor mad endeavour,
   Nor Man nor Boy,
Nor all that is at enmity with joy,
Can utterly abolish or destroy!
  Hence in a season of calm weather
   Though inland far we be,
Our Souls have sight of that immortal sea
   Which brought us hither,
  Can in a moment travel thither,
And see the Children sport upon the shore,
And hear the mighty waters rolling evermore.

X

Then sing, ye Birds, sing, sing a joyous song!
   And let the young Lambs bound
   As to the tabor's sound!
We in thought will join your throng,
  Ye that pipe and ye that play,
  Ye that through your hearts to-day
  Feel the gladness of the May!
What though the radiance which was once so bright
Be now for ever taken from my sight,
Though nothing can bring back the hour

Of splendour in the grass, of glory in the flower;
  We will grieve not, rather find
  Strength in what remains behind;
  In the primal sympathy
  Which having been must ever be;
  In the soothing thoughts that spring
  Out of human suffering;
  In the faith that looks through death,
In years that bring the philosophic mind.

XI

And O, ye Fountains, Meadows, Hills, and Groves,
Forebode not any severing of our loves!
Yet in my heart of hearts I feel your might;
I only have relinquished one delight
To live beneath your more habitual sway.
I love the Brooks which down their channels fret,
Even more than when I tripped lightly as they;
The innocent brightness of a new-born Day
  Is lovely yet;
The Clouds that gather round the setting sun
Do take a sober colouring from an eye
That hath kept watch o'er man's mortality;
Another race hath been, and other palms are won.
Thanks to the human heart by which we live,
Thanks to its tenderness, its joys, and fears,
To me the meanest flower that blows can give
Thoughts that do often lie too deep for tears.

      Hutchinson's Text

SIR HENRY WOTTON

100. On his Mistress, the Queen of Bohemia

You meaner beauties of the night,
That poorly satisfy our eyes,
More by your number, than your light,
You common people of the skies;
   What are you when the moon shall rise?

You curious chanters of the wood,
That warble forth Dame Nature's lays,
Thinking your passions understood
By your weak accents; what's your praise,
   When Philomel her voice shall raise?

You violets that first appear,
By your pure purple mantles known,
Like the proud virgins of the year,
As if the spring were all your own;
   What are you when the rose is blown?

So, when my mistress shall be seen
In form and beauty of her mind,
By virtue first, then choice, a Queen,
Tell me if she were not design'd
   Th'eclipse and glory of her kind?

1845 Edition

Printed in the USA
CPSIA information can be obtained
at www.ICGtesting.com
LVHW030359041023
760081LV00016B/295/J